COLLECTED TALES FROM A LONG ROOM

by the same author

THE STIRK OF STIRK
A TOUCH OF DANIEL
EXCEPT YOU'RE A BIRD
MOG
SHEMERELDA
I DIDN'T KNOW YOU CARED
TALES FROM A LONG ROOM
MORE TALES FROM A LONG ROOM
THE BRIGADIER FROM DOWN UNDER
THE BRIGADIER IN SEASON

COLLECTED TALES FROM A LONG ROOM

Peter Tinniswood

HUTCHINSON
London Melbourne Auckland Johannesburg

First published by Hutchinson & Co. Ltd in 1982
Reprinted in 1982
Reprinted in 1986

Hutchinson & Co. (Publishers) Ltd

An imprint of Century Hutchinson Ltd
Brookmount House, 62-65 Chandos Place, London WC2N 4NW

Century Hutchinson Publishing Group (Australia) Pty Ltd
16-22 Church Street, Hawthorn, Melbourne, Victoria 3122

Century Hutchinson Group (NZ) Ltd
32-34 View Road, PO Box 40-086, Glenfield, Auckland 10

Century Hutchinson Group (SA) (Pty) Ltd
PO Box 337, Bergvlei 2012, South Africa

Printed and bound in Great Britain by
Anchor Brendon Ltd, Tiptree, Essex

ISBN 0 09 150140 7

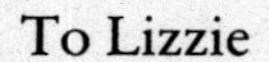

To Lizzie

Contents

Introduction

I was born in winter.

I love the summer.

My friend the Brigadier was born in Arlott St Johns.

He loves fine claret, Vimto, quail in season, barrage balloons, blotting paper, E. W. Swanson and his sister Gloria.

He recounted these tales to me during the course of a long and convivial summer spent in his favourite corner of a long room 'somewhere in England'.

Peter Tinniswood

1
Root's Boot

During the course of a long and arduous career in the service of King and country I have had the honour in the name of freedom and natural justice to slaughter and maim men (and women) of countless creeds and races.

Fuzzy wuzzies, Boers, Chinamen, Zulus, Pathans, Huns, Berbers, Turks, Japs, Gypos, Dagos, Wops and the odd Frog or two – all of them, no doubt, decent chaps 'in their own way'.

Who is to say, for example, that the Fuzzy Wuzzies don't have their equivalent of our own dear John Inman and the delicious Delia Smith, mother of the two Essex cricketing cousins, Ray and Peter?

I have no doubt that the Dagos have their counterpart

of our Anne Ziegler and Webster Booth, and I am perfectly certain that the Wops, just like us, have lady wives with hairy legs, loud voices and too many relations.

Indeed it is my firm opinion that all the victims of this carnage and slaughter were just like you and I – apart from their disgusting table manners and their revolting appearance.

Poor chaps, they had only two failings – they were foreigners and they were on the wrong side.

Now as I approach the twilight of my life I look back with pleasure and with pride on those campaigns which have brought me so much comfort and fulfilment – crushing the Boers at Aboukir Bay, biffing the living daylights out of the Turk at the Battle of Rorke's Drift, massacring the Aussies at The Oval in 1938.

But of all these battles one remains vividly in my mind to this very day – the Battle of Root's Boot.

The incidents pertaining to this conflict occurred in 1914 during the MCC's first and only tour to the Belgian Congo.

Who on earth had the crass stupidity to give the Congo to the Belgians in the first place is quite beyond me.

I am bound to say that I consider the Belgians to be the most revolting shower of people ever to tread God's earth.

Eaters of horse flesh, they let us down in two world wars. They're hopeless at golf. They drive on the wrong side of the road, and they're forever yodelling about their blasted fiords and their loathsome fretwork egg-timers.

Is it any wonder they made such a confounded mess of running the Congo?

When we went there in 1914, there was not one decent wicket the length and breadth of the country, and the facilities for nets were totally inadequate.

And, if that weren't enough, during our matches there were at least two outbreaks of cannibalism among spectators, which I found totally unacceptable, and which I am convinced were responsible for the loss of our most promising young leg spinner, M.M. Rudman-Stott.

He was sent out to field at deep third man in the match against an Arab Slavers' Country Eleven, and all we found of him after the tea interval was the peak of his Harlequins cap and half an indelible pencil.

But of these setbacks we were blissfully unaware as in high good spirits we set off from Liverpool in April 1914 aboard the steamship, SS *Duleepsinjhi*.

The party was skippered by the Rev. Thurston Salthouse-Bryden, a former chaplain to Madame Tussauds and a forceful if erratic opening bat who distinguished himself in 1927 playing for the Convocation of Canterbury by scoring a century before matins in the match against a Coptic Martyrs Eleven.

I had the honour to be vice captain and OC ablutions, and among the notable players in our midst were the Staffordshire opening bowler, Thunderton-Cartwright, who was later to become rugby league correspondent for *The Lancet*, and the number three bat and occasional seamer, Ashton, F., who was later responsible for the choreography of the Royal Ballet's highly acclaimed production of *Wisden's Almanack*, 1929, featuring

Alicia Markova as Ernest Tyldesley.

Of all the players in the party, though, the one who made the profoundest impression on all who met him (and some who didn't) was the all-rounder, Arthur Root, a distant cousin of the Derbyshire, Worcestershire and England player, Fred Root, of the same name.

Root was what we in the 'summer game' call 'a natural'.

During the voyage he kept us constantly entertained with his reading in Derbyshire dialect of the works of Colette, and his rendition on spoons and stirrup pumps of the later tone poems of Frederick Delius.

Root had charm, wit, erudition and the largest pair of feet it has ever been my privilege to encounter.

Indeed on the outward voyage they were directly responsible for saving the life of a Goanese steward who fell overboard seven nautical miles sou' sou' east of Ushant.

The poor wretch was applying linseed oil to the Rev. Salthouse-Bryden's self-righting lectern when a freak giant wave washed him overboard.

With the lifebelts being in use for a rumbustious game of deck quoits, Root with great presence of mind threw the only object available to him into the sea – to wit, his right boot.

The dusky Indian steward clambered into the pedicular container and was instantly hauled aboard by the boot laces.

Little did we realize then how vital that boot was to be to our safety and well-being many many months later.

We disembarked without incident at Matadi and set

off forthwith for the interior.

What a noble sight our native bearers made as they trudged along the primitive jungle trails carrying on their woolly heads the essential paraphernalia of our expedition – sight screens, portable scorebox and heavy roller.

The capital city, Leopoldville, was reached in three weeks.

How strange it was to our English eyes – no tram conductors, no Bedlington terriers, no Ordnance Survey bench marks.

Our only consolation came when Root discovered the local branch of Gunn and Moore's where we bought leopard-skin cricket bags, scorebooks bound in genuine okapi hide, and the Rev. Salthouse-Bryden purchased an object warranted as a Bantu baptismal love token, but which to my untutored eyes looked more like H. M. Stanley's left testicle.

We won each of our four matches in Leopoldville by an innings and 'a substantial margin', the Belgians ground fielding, as we had anticipated, being of a typically abysmal level.

A nation of congenital butterfingers, the Belgians.

We then set out for what was to be the most difficult and dangerous opposition of our entire tour – three unofficial Test matches against the Pygmies.

We left Leopoldville on a sultry August morning and did not reach our destination until late November 1914.

During the long and onerous trek we had the misfortune to lose three members of our party:

Evans-Pritchard, E. E.: stung by scorpion.

Leakey, L. S. B.: trampled by buffalo.

Attenborough, D.: retired hurt.

It was a nuisance to lose two wicket-keepers and a 'more than adequate' middle order batsman in that fashion, but nonetheless our party was in good spirits, when we arrived at Potto Potto to be greeted by officials of the Pygmy Board of Cricket Control.

The chairman, a gnarled, wizened little creature, who, incidentally, bore a marked resemblance to the distinguished light comedy actor and chanteuse, Mr John Inman, made us most welcome, offering us victuals and a choice of his most beautiful wives.

'Just like playing for Derby against Notts at Worksop,' said Root, and one and all joined in his hearty and innocent laughter.

On the advice of the Rev. Salthouse-Bryden we declined the feminine offerings but accepted the victuals which were served in the great adobe, thatched pavilion by elderly matrons of the tribe.

It was during the subsequent revelries that the first hitch in the proceedings occurred.

By prior arrangement we were to provide the balls to be used in the match, and, as a matter of courtesy, our baggage master, Swanton, presented a box of same to be examined by the Pygmy officials.

Imagine our horror when the minute, dark-skinned fraternity passed the balls from hand to hand, sniffed them, shook them and, with expressions of sublime delight, ate them.

Worse was to follow when the severely truncated tinted gents offered us the balls they wished to use – row upon row of small spherical objects, gnarled, matted, wrinkled and pitted.

For a moment we gazed at them in stunned silence.

Then the Rev. Salthouse-Bryden exclaimed:

'Saints preserve us – they are shrunken heads.'

What could have been the very severest of fraught situations was saved by our ever-genial giant, Root.

Picking up one of the heads in his massive fist, he examined it briefly and then said:

'Don't worry, skipper. We'll use this 'un. It should be just right for seaming after lunch.'

The day of the first unofficial test dawned bright and clear.

The Pygmies won the toss and elected to bat.

The two Pygmy openers made their way to the wicket to the accompaniment of the howling of monkeys and the screeching of gaudily feathered parakeets, and as I watched them take the crease from my vantage point at deep extra cover, it was for all the world like looking through the wrong end of a pair of binoculars at a dusky wee George Wood and an extremely sunburned Mr Harry Pilling.

Our opening bowler, Thunderton-Cartwright, came bounding to the wicket to deliver the first ball of this historic match.

It whistled from his hand at ferocious pace.

But all to no avail.

On the puddingy and unresponsive pitch the ball thudded mutely into the turf and rose no more than six inches from the ground.

'Bouncer,' yelled the Pygmy opener.

It was a cry taken up in unison by the masses of minuscule spectators packed in dense masses in what was, I believe, their equivalent of the Warner Stand.

An ugly incident seemed certain to ensue.

But at that moment, totally unexpected, came the crackle of small arms fire, and across the distant river burst a column of native Askaris.

As the Askaris waded across the river, firing indiscriminately from the hip, the Pygmies fled as if by magic.

As bullets whistled past our ears we flung ourselves to the ground, only to hear the following words which plunged an icy dagger to the depths of our hearts.

'On your feet, Englische Schweinhunds!'

We looked up to see three white men, dressed in khaki drill, with shaven heads and leering duelling scars upon their cheeks.

'Huns,' we cried in unison.

Indeed they were.

Why hadn't MCC informed us that war had been declared?

Why hadn't the Test and County Cricket Board notified us that marauding parties of German colonial troops were rampaging through the territory?

Why was there no news in *The Cricketer* of the conflagration that was to rewrite the map of Europe and suspend for four years all Test matches between England and Australia?

Such thoughts flashed through my mind as we were bound by the straps of our cricket pads to the portable scoreboard, and the Askaris lined themselves in front of us in firing squad formation.

It was then, as death stared us in the face, that we were addressed by our skipper, the Rev. Salthouse-Bryden.

'Oh, Lord,' he said. 'Thou hast in Thy wisdom decreed that our innings shall be closed.

'It is pleasing to Thine eye that in that great score-book in the sky it shall be written of our party, "Death stopped play".

'So, Lord, give us the strength to face the long walk back to the celestial pavilion like men and members of the MCC, or whichever is more appropriate.'

It was at that moment that I noticed that Root was improperly dressed for the occasion.

His right boot was missing.

Before I could speak he motioned with his eyes towards the distant river.

An amazing sight met my eyes.

Floating silently in the current was a large right cricket boot.

And in it, paddling silently, was a war party of our erstwhile Pygmy opponents.

The Huns and Askaris, totally unaware of the approaching sporting footwear, paused to gloat over their triumph.

It was to be their undoing, for in an instant the boot touched the river bank, the Pygmies sprang out through the lace holes and, screaming like dervishes, unloosed their poisoned arrows against them.

It was all over in seconds.

The Askaris and their vile Teutonic masters lay dead at our feet.

The match was resumed the following morning.

We had the good fortune to win, when Root took the last three Pygmy wickets with the last three balls of the match.

Years later he was to maintain that this was only possible owing to the slight inconsistency in the second new ball, which caused him to produce prodigious variations in swing and bounce.

And with a smile and a gentle nod of his genial head he would say:

'I reckon it were the duelling scar in the seam what done it.'

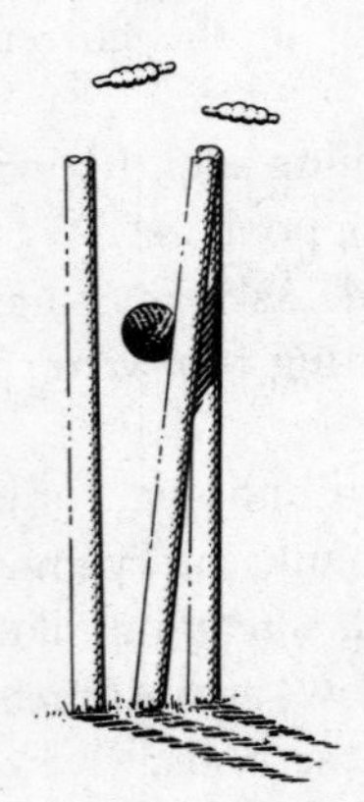

2
Our Own Dear Queen

It is a fact not generally known that in her youth Queen Victoria had the makings of a cricketer of considerable stature.

Indeed it is the opinion of many historians of the 'summer game' that but for the cares of state and the burdens of excessive childbearing, she could well have reached Test match standard.

Contemporary records reveal that the young Victoria was endowed with an excess of the cricketing virtues – the athletic grace of a Frank Woolley, the snow-white teeth of a Learie Constantine, the combative pugnacity of a Freddie Trueman, the dark, hairy legs of a W. G. Grace.

There are many experts who firmly believe that after her death Queen Victoria achieved reincarnation in the form of Mr George Duckworth of Lancashire and England.

While the resemblance, facially and vocally, cannot be denied, I myself tend to the view that, if reincarnation did take place, it came in the shape of Mr B. D. 'Bomber' Wells of Gloucestershire and Nottinghamshire.

His broad beam and the slow waddle to the wicket before delivery of the ball always seemed to me to have a regal quality that was not to be explained by Altham coaching manual, but bore all the hallmarks of a person well used to the state opening of colonial parliaments and the rigours of nineteenth-century confinement and pregnancy.

Dear 'Bomber' Wells!

How different the history of our beloved country and, indeed the wide world beyond, might have been had he acceded to the throne in 1837 – though I am bound to say I have slight doubts about his ability to cope with the demands of Prince Albert of Saxe-Coburg-Gotha.

This odious German princeling has in my view cast a dark, malign shadow over this country, which to this very day has still to be lifted.

How else to explain the benighted summer of 1980 with its long and dreary succession of rain-affected county cricket matches, its dripping sight screens, its sodden squares and its elevation to the prime ministership of a woman with the manners of an ink monitor and the charm of a power-mad swimming baths attendant?

How else indeed?

I believe passionately that most of the great calamities of this century can legitimately be placed at the feet of this nauseous German princeling – the loss of Empire, the decline of pride and patriotism, the enfeebling of manly courage and vigour, the demise of the leg spinner, the retirement from the *Daily Telegraph* of Mr E. W. Swanton, father and grandfather respectively of that celebrated Hollywood film star, Miss Gloria Swanton.

Do I exaggerate? Do I overstate my case?

I think not.

Consider this.

Had this country been ruled in its pomp and in its prime by a monarch who had played Test match cricket, opened the innings for her country at Headingley, been struck in the ribs by Spofforth at The Oval, smashed in the teeth by Gregory at Old Trafford, bitten on the buttocks by the groundsman's ferrets at Trent Bridge, is it conceivable that Britain should be in its present desperate plight with women newsreaders on the moving television screens and threatened centre-page pin-ups of Brian Johnston in *Wisden's Almanack*?

Nothing will dissuade me from the opinion that had Queen Victoria been allowed to develop her cricketing ability to its fullest potential, this dear country of ours would still be 'mistress of the seas', 'mother of the free' and holders *in perpetuum* of the Corbillon Cup.

And what relevance has Prince Albert to this?

The answer is simple.

He it was who forbad his wife, his youthful, fresh and innocent bride, from wielding the willow, donning the pads and weaving her subtle spells with the crimson rambler.

Let us consider the facts calmly and objectively. The historical canon relates that Queen Victoria first met her putative consort at Windsor on 10 October 1839.

This is not, in fact, the case.

In an appendix omitted in somewhat mysterious circumstances from Heygarth's *Scores and Biographies* there is a reference to a cricket match held in June 1838 at Crabbe Park, in which Queen Victoria, playing for William Blunt's Eleven, took seven wickets for seven runs and struck three successive sixes off the redoubtable F. W. Lillywhite.

She scored an undefeated 87 in 23 minutes, the ferocity of her hitting being only matched many years later by Mr G. L. Jessop, and the fluency of her stroke play having no equal until the arrival of 'the silken-shirted Hindu', Mr K. S. Ranjitsinjhi, whose descendants incidently now run a most agreeable Tandoori chicken restaurant on the outskirts of Keating New Town.

Unknown to our so-called academic historians, with their limp bow ties and discoloured waistcoats, Prince Albert was in the close vicinity of the cricket ground engaged in business of a quite different nature.

He was on an unofficial visit to this country, examining and evaluating the latest developments in animal husbandry and land management.

It was while he was in a neighbouring field inspecting a novel and amusing device for the instant decapitation of poachers that he was struck a violent blow behind the left temple by a ball smitten out of the ground over deep square leg by Queen Victoria.

He was knocked unconscious.

On regaining his senses he inquired as to the nature of the blow which had caused an irregular egg-shaped protruberance to appear on his close-cropped, bullet-shaped cranial extremity.

'Lord save us, sir,' said the farmer. 'Tis the Queen what done it. It must be her batting. The stumper is standing up at the wicket.'

There and then Albert resolved to marry the young Victoria, daughter of Edward, Duke of Kent, niece of Leopold, first King of the Belgians, and devoted drinking companion of Mr Fuller Pilch.

Why did he make this decision?

I believe that at the very moment the leather-bound sphere struck his temple there was released in him all those primeval stirrings of violence, bestiality and brutality inherent in the soul of every Hun who ever lived.

A woman who could inflict pain!

A woman who could knock unconscious a man in the prime of his life!

She must be his.

Nothing less could satisfy the loathsome yearnings of his black Teutonic heart.

The marriage took place on 10 February 1840.

The *Encyclopaedia Britannica* states that the Queen was 'dressed entirely in articles of British manufacture'.

This was indeed the case.

For under her dress of purest Macclesfield silk she wore Gunn and Moore cricket pads, Daymart thermal string vest and Gray-Nicolls abdominal protector made out of stout Sheffield steel and covered with the tartan of the Gordon Highlanders.

Later that evening in the bridal chamber as the young Queen commenced to disrobe, the Prince was enchanted by what, to his untutored eye, was the novelty of this garb.

The sensuous slap of cricket pads against chaste and pristine flesh as his new bride practised her off drive, the tumble of silken hair over smooth young shoulders as she removed her I Zingari cricket cap, the faint, exotic whiff of Sloane's liniment as she wheeled over her arm in that distinctive 'square on' delivery style aroused in him strange, exciting and not unwelcome feelings of desire in the nether regions of his popping crease.

It was with a happy and pumping heart that he retired to his nuptial bed.

Imagine his chagrin when his young bride insisted on taking a net before joining him in the conjugal container.

It is my belief that the humiliations he suffered that honeymoon night contributed more than anything else to his subsequent gravity of mien, his humourless, grinding, rigid code of morals and his ceaseless and finally successful efforts to stop the young queen's cricketing activities.

Picture the scene that honeymoon night.

The young bride crouches at the wicket.

The young groom, clad in night shirt and velvet smoking hat, trots stiffly to the wicket.

And in his first three deliveries bowls two long hops and a daisy cutter.

Could any man suffer greater humiliation on his wedding night?

Could anything be more designed to strengthen his will to turn his ebullient, feckless and vivacious young spouse into the authoritarian, dour and austere woman, whose devotion to the duties of state and childbearing was awesome in its comprehensiveness?

Nine children!

No wonder she had such trouble with her run up.

But let us consider the reasons for this prodigality of progeny in greater detail.

Was it really the full and riotous flowering of the maternal instinct?

Was it, in fact, something more than the altruistic desire to provide spouses for a whole legion of European kings, archdukes and landgraves, whose descendants to this very day are to be seen bathing topless without togs on the beaches of southern France and providing their endorsements to the boards of loathsome companies engaged in the manufacture of microwave ovens and digital toenail clippers?

I think so.

Let the dark facts speak for themselves.

It is historically indisputable that after her marriage Queen Victoria refused steadfastly to abandon her cricketing proclivities.

Despite all her husband's despotic discipline she was frequently to be seen opening the batting incognito for Quidnuncs and the Free Foresters, carousing in the back parlour of The Bat and Ball at Hambledon and pulling the heavy roller with 'the best of them' at the White Hart Hotel in Bromley.

In vain did Prince Albert remonstrate with her.

In vain did he appeal to her sense of responsibility

and duty.

There was only one thing for him to do.

Involve her in a constant succession of pregnancies.

This he did, secure in the knowledge that no man in the history of the 'summer game' had ever played Test cricket successfully after the third month of pregnancy.

His plan was propitious.

By the time of his death Queen Victoria's cricketing activities had entirely ceased and her beloved Gray-Nicolls abdominal protector lay rusting in an obscure and dark corner of the royal mews and her prized Geoffrey Boycott autograph cricket bat was relegated to ceremonial duties at the Tower of London.

When I now think of our dear Queen's long reign, I do not think of a monarch who saw vast tracts of the atlas shaded pink and the creation of an Empire on which the sun never set.

No, I think of and mourn the passing of a lady who could, had her immense talents and inclinations been allowed to run their natural course, have been the finest all-round cricketer of her generation and, when age took its inevitable toll, could have developed into an umpire of the most outstanding calibre.

Who is to say, in fact, that she has not already achieved that eminence in the personage of Mr Bill Alley?

3
The Ditherers

Of all the happy memories I cherish from my long association with the 'summer game', some of the most precious spring from carefree days spent in the company of The Ditherers.

History does not recount when this touring cricket club was established.

It is well known, however, that from its earliest days it has always had the closest and most cordial military, colonial and thespian associations.

Its presence has been recorded in accounts of the Peninsular War, when a group of British officers, taking a net at the lines of Torres Vedres, was surprised by a squadron of Walloon irregular cavalry and massacred for the loss of all ten wickets.

Contemporary Chinese silk prints of the period seem to suggest that The Ditherers played a number of matches during the Boxer Rebellion.

Indeed one of the characters depicted, dressed in surgical sandals, wincyette cummerbund and Free Foresters' thermal underwear, bears a marked resemblance to the distinguished theatrical producer, Sir Peter Hall, brother of the equally distinguished West Indian Test cricketer, Wes.

It was a few years later during a tour to the Trucial States that The Ditherers' deputy stumper was captured by Arab slavers and was not seen again until the early 1930s when an MCC raiding party discovered him in the court of a minor Saudi princeling, where he occupied the position of chief scorer to the royal harem.

Despite his protestations he was bound and gagged and smuggled back to England in the false bottom of a Slazenger cricket bag.

For many years until his death he was to be seen, a lonely and bedraggled figure, skulking in shop doorways in the vicinity of the headquarters of the Ladies' Netball Association of Great Britain.

It was around this time that I began my long and happy association with The Ditherers.

I was staying with relations at the picturesque Lancashire village of Cardus-in-Ribblesdale when The Ditherers arrived to play the local cricket team.

Unfortunately, a series of accidents, involving among others, an infected cricket bat and a rumbustious evening with members of the Rochdale Hornets Ladies rugby league team, had much depleted their numbers.

Much to my delight I was invited by their skipper, the young Glamorgan 'leg tweaker', Ivor Novello, to play for them, and, going in last man down, had the pleasure of both scoring the winning run and taking our side's score into double figures.

Thus began five decades of 'cricket wandering', which has taken me to some of the most enchanting and magical spots on the face of the earth and given me a treasure chest full of fond recollections of fellow tourists, both military and theatrical.

How well I remember that blissful tour of Albania, when Elsie and Doris Waters notched an unbeaten opening partnership of 234.

How well I recall that tour of Greece, when Noel Coward played havoc with Eleven Gentlemen of Athens.

He also performed quite adequately on the cricket field, too.

Still etched on my memory is our tour of Southern India, when for five solid weeks the whole party was laid low with the most violent attack of the Nawab of Pataudis. (On reflection I think that 'solid' is not the most appropriate of words to describe those five weeks of agony.)

That apart, nothing can erase from my mind's eye the picture of the future saviour of civilization as we know it, Lord Mountbatman, saving our match against Bangkok Brotheliers in a last wicket partnership with Mrs Simpson, future Duchess of Windsor and mother of the Australian Test skipper, Bobby.

If, however, I were asked to name my most precious souvenir of my membership of The Ditherers, I would be compelled to say that it was the friendship I formed with our baggage master, Wisbeach.

Ernest Henry Bismark Wisbeach was what we in the 'summer game' call 'a character'.

His physical appearance suggested someone who had spent a great deal of his youth teaching greyhounds how to cheat at racing, and his manner suggested one whose adolescence had been spent in the company of Mafia hit men, Corsican bandits and Yorkshire opening bowlers.

Wisbeach was a man of 'many parts'.

In addition to his talents for farmyard impersonations and forgery, he was also a considerable poet 'in his own right'.

He it was who penned those memorable lines, which seemed to encapsulate all that was most noble and manly from the carnage and horror of the First World War:

I seen a Hun.
He had a gun.
I run.

He was also a noted purveyor of pithy and pungent graffiti.

One of the finest examples of his work was created during The Ditherers' tour of Vienna in the mid-1930s.

It is to be seen in the urinals of the Staatsoper and runs as follows:

'Mozart is a wanker.'

Underneath, written in typical German script, someone has added the legend:

'And so is Emmott Robinson.'

Despite Wisbeach's reputation for unwarranted beligerence, foul table manners and personal uncleanliness, I myself always found him to be a most loyal, entertaining and diverting travelling companion.

In fact, I think I can say without immodesty that he took a shine to me immediately on our first meeting.

This friendship was cemented during The Ditherers' visit to Paris in 1935, when by an unfortunate chain of circumstances, which to this day are too painful to recall, I found myself incarcerated in prison wrapped in a horse blanket and having in my possession a black velvet garter, a bent bulldog clip and the left lapel of Mr Leslie Sarony's smoking jacket.

Wisbeach it was who extricated me from this predicament. I never asked how.

He did not encourage discussion on this matter, although he seemed well satisfied with the annuity of several hundred pounds he insisted I assign to him immediately after my release from prison.

Many people have asked me how it was that Wisbeach, considering his total incompetence as a baggage master, managed to hold down his job with The Ditherers for so many years.

I am bound to confess that he was indeed deplorably deficient in the execution of his duties.

Without any difficulty whatsoever I can recall disasters involving the loss of our portable heavy roller and horse on the Simplon-Orient Express in 1932, the loss of nineteen sets of cricket bats and a crate of Cooper's Oxford marmalade during the tour of Peru and the loss of Oscar Rabin and Miss Shirley Abicair during the tour of the Andaman Islands.

No, I am as baffled about Wisbeach's continuing

employment as all the other members of The Ditherers, most of whom, coincidently, I discovered many years later, appeared to be paying annuities of one sort or another to our erstwhile baggage master.

Most curious.

But nowhere near as curious as Wisbeach's behaviour and subsequent disappearance during The Ditherers' tour to America in 1939.

As always on these occasions Wisbeach insisted on making all the travel arrangements himself.

Our Hon. Sec. had in the past complained about this, but on being taken into a corner by Wisbeach and whispered to in the most conspiratorial and threatening of manner had always withdrawn his objections with a rapidity which to this very day I still find extraordinary in the extreme.

Still, despite our forebodings about the travel arrangements, we were all in high good spirits as we arrived at Liverpool in the late summer of 1939 looking forward with the keenest anticipation to a crossing of the Atlantic by Cunarder.

Imagine our horror when we discovered that the vessel in which we were to cross 'the briney' was not a noble ocean liner, but a foul-smelling, rust-streaked tramp steamer, the SS *Bernard Manning*.

Our accommodation, too, I am bound to say, fell far short of our expectations.

I never really fully mastered the art of climbing into my hammock in cricket pads and protector, and during the storms which increased in ferocity as the voyage progressed, life in our communal lower decks cabin grew hazardous in the extreme as the cricket balls, which had broken loose from their packing case, whirred about our heads like howitzer shells.

We were puzzled, too, on our first night at sea to find Wisbeach dining at the captain's table while we were consigned to an exceptionally unstable trestle table in the darkest recesses of the dining saloon.

However, as the great E. R. Dexter once wrote most perceptively, 'Every cloud has a silver lining'. The ship began to pitch and toss and yaw in the most frightful manner and we were all given invaluable slip fielding practice as we endeavoured to catch the ship's biscuits, which flew from our enamel plates in every direction.

That night as we huddled in our cabin, blessing the tarpaulin covers we had borrowed from the Oval and under which we sheltered, we considered our plight.

What to do?

Mutiny was mooted, but when reflecting upon the plight of numerous Yorkshire cricket professionals who had taken similar action, this notion was swiftly abandoned.

Our specialist cover point suggested mass suicide.

This had its attractions to us all, but when our skipper pointed out that such action might adversely affect our membership of MCC, this notion, too, was abandoned.

No, there was nothing to do but 'grin and bear it'.

For the next six days the conditions of our existence bordered on the intolerable.

Three sets of nets were washed overboard before we had even time to tack our matting wicket to the deck.

Our portable score-box was smashed to smithereens where it stood on the port side davits.

Our first choice opening bats, Dame Flora Robson

and Dame Anna Neagle, had in extremes of terror taken refuge in the crow's nest and, despite the entreaties of our utility off-spinner, Mr Victor Sylvester (leader Mr Oscar Grasso) refused to come down.

Our misery was complete.

On the evening of the seventh day, however, our fortunes changed in the most drastic manner.

We had only been locked in our cabin for ten minutes when, quite without warning, the wind abated and the seas assumed a still, deathless calm.

We looked at each other in astonishment.

Our amazement was instantly increased when the ship's engines stopped.

Then high above us we heard footsteps on the upper decks and the ship's siren hooted softly three times.

In an instant our stumper, Miss Ethel Revnell, hoisted Mr Nosmo King upon her broad shoulders and instructed him to look out of the porthole and report on what he saw.

His subsequent monologue caused us to gasp in wonderment.

Its essence was as follows:

In the sylphlike beams of the moon he saw a boat being lowered from the side of our ship.

It was rowed by four sturdy seamen.

And, standing upright in its stern sheets was – yes, it was Wisbeach.

But whither was that boat bound?

The answer was swift to present itself.

A creaming of waters.

A snarling of muffled engines.

And then out of the salty depths appeared, with water

streaming from its flanks, a submarine.

No.

A U-boat.

(At this juncture Lord Baden-Powell collapsed in a dead swoon, inflicting terminal damage on his woggle.)

Our ship's boat crew drew alongside the German warship and, wonder of wonders, Wisbeach stepped aboard.

And the last Mr Nosmo King, or indeed any of us, saw of our baggage master was his distinctive figure standing upright in the U-boat's conning tower, his right arm held stiffly aloft and pointing at the moon.

Our tour of America was not a success.

I often wonder if our playing record might have been different had we not spent seventeen days in open boats after the German U-boat torpedoed our vessel.

I often wonder, too, what became of Wisbeach.

There are those who maintained that he was appointed baggage master to the German Afrika Korps in the Western Desert, pointing to the fact that in papers left after his death there is proof that Rommel was paying an annuity of £230 per annum to Wisbeach.

I myself take a more charitable view.

I believe that he was, in fact, a secret agent sent by MCC to assassinate Adolf Hitler, but with typical incompetence he failed in his mission, and the Führer survives to this very day in the form of Mr Kerry Packer.

4
'Backstop'

It is my proud boast to say that I have read and indeed known many of the finest scribes and writers associated with our great 'summer game'.

How the names trip off the tongue: Neville Cardew, R. C. Robertson-Hare, Bruce Woodcock of *The Times*, who achieved greater fame early in his career as a pugilist of distinction, and E. W. Swanson, father and brother respectively of that uniquely glamorous star of the moving kinematograph, Miss Gloria Arlott.

But none of these celebrated writers in my opinion compares in style, in wit, in vision and in depth of knowledge with 'Backstop'.

What pleasure beyond compare he gave to countless

generations of 'old sweats' as we served King and country in one of the farthest and most unprepossessing outposts of the British Empire.

I have no hesitation in saying that without 'Backstop' the *Rangoon Weekly Clarion and Trumpeter* would have been just another 'rag'.

Antony had his Cleopatra, Callard had his Bowser, Goethe had his Daisy, Eddie Waring had his Gillow – and so did the *Clarion and Trumpeter* have its 'Backstop'.

How eagerly we awaited delivery of that journal in those scented tropic evenings, serenaded by the languid whirr of the punkah, the muted duskings of monkey chatter and the steady, comforting rasp of our lady wives shaving their armpits.

The routine was ever the same.

Friday evening. The week's labours over. Pink gin. Quinine tablets at hand to ward off the inevitable post-curry attack of the dreaded Nawab of Pataudis.

And on to the verandah would pad our faithful Indian jock-strap wallah, Umrigar, his innocent liquid brown eyes beaming with pleasure as grovelling on hands and knees he would present us clenched in his snow-white teeth the latest copy of our beloved *Clarion and Trumpeter*.

I would wrench the rolled-up newspaper from his oriental dental impedimenta and in an ecstacy of delight belabour him about the head and shoulders in a manner which his descendants were to find all too familiar in an encounter with Mr F. S. Trueman many years later in 1952.

Then, dismissing the wretch with an affectionate cuff

round the popping crease, I would seat myself on my Frindall patent portable umpire's commode and settle myself down to an evening's reading.

Ah, the bliss.

Joy unbounded withstanding even the presence of the lady wife staring at me unblinkingly with her piggy little eyes as she knitted another of her interminable muslin trench comforters for her supercilious pet macaw, Dexter.

A quick flick through the pages of the newspaper and there on the back page he would be revealed in all his glory – 'Backstop', a haven of old England in a storm of unspeakable alien loathsomeness.

To me and to many like me, 'Backstop' was the epitome of home in all its nostalgic glory. One had only to read the briefest of his highly distinctive prose to be transported instantly to the damp depths of a London 'pea souper' or the sullen plod of shire horses through cloying Cheshire loam.

I am reminded of those far-off days now as I sit in my study.

The gas fire stutters, the home-bound rooks loiter across a lowering sky, the stuffed cárcases of Dexter gazes down on me icily from his perch on top of the television set, and I rustle through my old, fading and yellowing copies of the *Rangoon Weekly Clarion and Trumpeter*.

What memories it brings back to me as my eyes wander over the front page and the close-printed lists of small ads.

'For sale – one Nepalese ballroom dancer.'

'Serious gentleman with pointed teeth seeks mature

lady with similar interests.'

'Tall jockey seeks position with very large horse.'

'Home bible readings and colonic irrigation. Reply in strictest confidence to the Rev. G. A. R. Lock.'

I turn over the front page and the following evocative headline springs out to soothe and comfort my tired old eyes:

'By tandem and canoe to the upper reaches of the Irrawaddy.

'An account of "An Adventure" by the Misses Compton and Edrich.'

Dear Miss Compton.

How chaste, how pious, how refined.

How tragic she should end her days in a fatal accident with a jar of Brylcream.

Onwards, ever onwards, I flick through the pages.

'Recent Arrivals at Rangoon on the steamship, *Duleepsinjhi*.

'Surgeon General K. R. Cranston to relieve Mr Pollard as Principal Dental Consultant to Indigenous Shans.

'Col. and Mrs Washbrook to take up appointment with the Inspectorate of Irrigation and Sightscreens, Mandalay.

'The Hon. W. Place en route to Rawtenstall.'

The pages rustle.

My eyes croon to blurred photographs of slim young ladies in flowing white dresses and khaki shin pads, of bandits strung from wayside gibbets, of the haggard faces of dissident Yorkshire professionals banished to the jungles during the mercifully distant savage regime of Ghengis Sellars.

A salty tear trickles from my eye and falls upon page 19 and : 'Simple Recipes for Simple Servants. Number 863. Boiled cricket ball with linseed gravy.'

And now for the last page.

With what anticipation my trembling hands turn over the newspaper.

There.

There it is.

The headline.

'Gentlemen of Burma versus Mr Arthur Gilligan's Eleven of the MCC.'

Ah, memories.

Sweet memories.

But wait!

What is this beneath the headline?

'Owing to unfortunate indisposition, the report of this match has not been compiled by 'Backstop'. At extremely short notice his place has been taken by Rear Admiral Sir Henry Blofeld. We apologise for the resultant hyperbole and litotes.'

Good God.

I remember.

I remember it well.

Let me compose myself and search through the dusty lofts of memory to recall an incident which even now as I dribble whisky down my lap and spill gentleman's relish over the dozing cat brings pain and darkness to my brow.

Let us begin at the beginning.

Let us try to picture the scene at the turn of the century as the young 'Backstop' disembarks from the steamship *Nayudu* at Rangoon.

What does he carry in that battered Gladstone bag and the tin trunk with the rusted flanks?

Beribboned letters from a broken-hearted lover perchance?

A fond mother's portrait in a silver frame?

A treasured fragment of 'Monkey' Hornby's underpants?

Who can tell?

What fears and forebodings pump to the core of that sensitive soul as he sets off into the interior to take up employ as assistant left luggage supervisor with the Grand Central fully authorized and Harmonious Railway?

Who indeed can guess.

'Backstop' has left us no record of those early days in the wild Manipur Hills.

We can only imagine lonely evenings spent teaching Nagas the rudiments of swing and swerve, bleak, monsoon-bound Sundays instructing Kachins in the arts of scorebook compiling, fever-ridden nights of frustration as he endeavoured to impress upon sullen Chins the intricate subtleties of umpires' signals.

We have some evidence of his success in these matters.

In his memoirs of the Burma campaign relating how single-handedly and with one great bound he defeated the hordes of Nippon, the late and much-lamented Lord Mountbatman recalls how once towards the end of hostilities against the Japanese his aide-de-camp received a flesh wound in the right thigh from a stray oriental bullet.

As the aide-de-camp fell to the ground his Chin guide turned to His Lordship with a smile and with a fluent movement that would not have disgraced the great umpire, 'Cheerful' Charlie Chester, lifted his right leg, extended it sideways, tapped it violently with his right hand and held his left arm aloft.

'Damnit,' said Lord Mountbatman. 'The fellow's signalling a leg bye. Yet another example of the great and multifarious benefits I single-handedly and with one great bound have granted to the civilized world as I and a few privileged friends know it.'

How I wish 'Backstop' had been present to disabuse the noble Lord.

But, no, let us not deal with conjecture.

Let us confine ourselves to facts and assert that when 'Backstop' reappeared from his lonely sojourn in the Manipur Hills it was with the rank of Chief Inspector Buffers and Ticket Punchers.

He had with him a native wife, sixteen children of various hue, a deaf Bedlington terrier and a rusting tin leg, on which was stencilled in faded letters the legend 'Not Wanted On Voyage'.

He also had 'a problem'.

There are those who maintain that it was his wife who drove him to drink and to journalism.

As the whole history of newspapers is liberally littered with similar cases, I do not feel qualified to oppose this opinion.

Certainly his wife made a far from attractive impression with her brown, wizened skin, her treble chins, her strident voice, and the hectoring manner with which she addressed her husband – this again is an experience which many journalists of my acquaintance will not find unfamiliar.

If indeed his wife was responsible for 'Backstop's' problem, we can only lament his recourse to 'the demon'.

On the other hand we can only be posthumously grateful to that lady for her influence in introducing her spouse to the world of ink and quill.

For over ten years 'Backstop' graced the pages of the *Rangoon Weekly Clarion and Trumpeter* with his reports of cricketing campaigns.

The prose was ever immaculate, the style unique and the wit and polish unexampled.

There are those churlish spirits who point out that in some of his reports there were faint undertones of undesirable racial bias.

Poppycock.

Who but a prude and pedant of the basest sort could take exception to the following extract, which shows 'Backstop' in all his literary glory?

'Next to the wicket waddled the unmistakeably loathsome figure of the opponents' Burmese skipper.

'The slanted Mongoloid eyes, the greasy, olive skin, the typically untrustworthy shift of the shoulders, the plump, perspiring contours of over-indulgence and indolence proved no match for the noble and upright wiles of the prince of the lobsters, Simpson-Hayward.

'With a sneer to his lips and a contemptuous flick of the wrist the man from the rich and rolling shires of Worcester released the crimson rambler, which, describing a parabola of the most lissom of proportions, came to earth with a lustrous whisper on the smooth breast of green and with a sigh and a slough rose like a fond lover's mast seeking the fig-pink haven of his young bride's bower of pleasure and spat from a perfect full length to wreck the castle of the foul-smelling obsequious Oriental.'

Only a man who had written such resonant prose could have died happily on the morning of the match, Gentlemen of Burma versus Mr Arthur Gilligan's Eleven of the MCC.

Let us not dwell or linger on the circumstances of his untimely demise.

I myself can affirm that three hours before his 'call to glory' he left the premises of the Royal Burma Mounted Tricycle Club in the highest of good spirits.

The groundsman of the Rangoon Ramblers Cricket Club was to maintain forever that there was a smile on 'Backstop's' face as the heavy roller behind which he had taken a token nap in refuge from the heat of the blistering sun lumbered over his prostrate body.

All that was to be heard as the roller proceeded in its inexorable way was the faint sound of tinkling glass.

There are cynics who assert that this was the sound of splintering gin bottles.

I myself believe fervently, passionately, that it was the sound of the glass breaking on the autographed picture of Mr O.S. Nock, which he had carried constantly on his person since his early days with the railway in the Manipur Hills.

Only one thing marred his death.

At the subsequent post mortem when the pathologist opened up his tin leg, it was found to contain battered copies of *Wisden's Almanacks*, 1902-13.

Fortunately 'Backstop's' reputation remained unsullied.

He was indeed fortunate to have friends 'in high places' who were able to suppress the information that it was 'Backstop' himself who had, during his years in the wilderness, masterminded the operation which had come so perilously close to destroying the whole fabric of the British occupation of Burma.

I refer, of course, to the smuggling of *Wisden's Almanacks* to the impressionable and innocent subject peoples of the darkest interior.

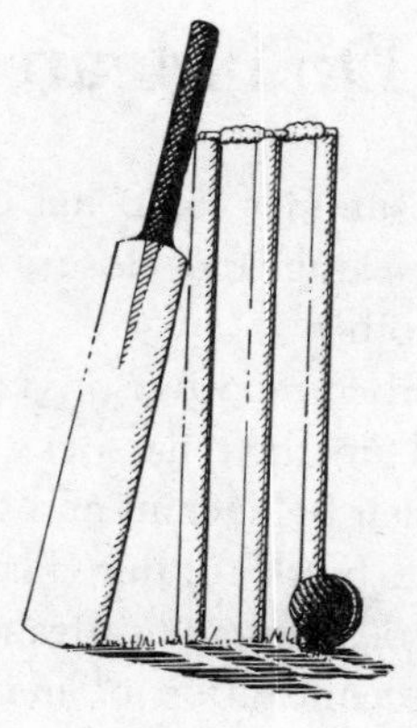

5
What Do I Mean By?

The history of our 'summer game' has been constantly distinguished by its long and close association with 'gentlemen of the cloth'.

How many bucolic country parsons have strapped on their pads, hitched up their hassocks, adjusted their fanons, blancoed their baldachins and strode out on to the cricket field to do battle for thir village team?

How many rural deacons and suffragen bishops have officiated at the solemnization of marriages and the dedication of new lifeboats while secretly wearing under their robes their Free Forester's underpants?

The first-class game, too, has been graced by the appearance of clerics, both humble and distinguished.

A glance at Wisden will reveal that His Holiness, George Pope, gave noble service to the county of Derbyshire for many, many years.

More recently that portly and amiable cricketer, David Shepherd, on his retirement from Gloucestershire county cricket club was appointed Bishop of Liverpool.

And, in my opinion, not before time.

My thoughts have strayed in this direction after recently attending a service at the parish church of St Wilfred, the blessed Rhodes.

The padre there is an old friend of mine.

His name is the Rev. A. K. Mole-Drably, and it is my custom every year to attend the service designated in the Book of Common Prayer as 'The Third Sunday after the Lords Test'.

The church itself is splendid, built in the 'early Headingley' style with its exquisite reredos made from the remains of the sight-screens at Bramall Lane and its magnificent stained-glass windows depicting scenes in the life of Emmott Robinson.

Mole-Drably, a cricket fanatic all his life, took up the living of St Wilfred, the blessed Rhodes, after serving several years as chaplain-general to Sealink.

It was while conducting a service on *The Maid of Orleans* that he achieved episcopal immortality as the only man ever to be seasick while giving holy communion to Mr Wilfred Wooller.

Fortunately for him, Wooller decided not to excommunicate him, a typical act of Christian charity by this near-saintly man, whose name is revered the length and breadth of his native Wales and indeed is the object of cult worship by some of the more primitive peoples of the upper Swansea valley.

It was Mole-Drably's abiding interest in our 'summer game' that was ultimately responsible for his taking over the incumbency of St Wilfred, the blessed Rhodes.

The incident occurred during the annual international cricker *eisteddfod* at Colwyn Bay, when Mole-Drably was acting as umpire in the match Church in Wales Select versus Wynford Vaughan-Thomas.

A chance meeting during the luncheon adjournment with the archbishop of Canterbury, who at that time was Mr E. W. Swanton, later to achieve even greater ecclesiastical eminence as chief cricket writer for the *Daily Telegraph*, was instrumental in Mole-Drably's transference from his maritime ministrations to the quieter backwaters of sacerdotal suburbia.

His Blessed and Overwhelming Reverence E. W. Swanton was leaving the main pavilion where he had been viewing an exibition of Mr Tony Lewis's letters of application to join the National Union of Journalists and listening to a recital of early Carmarthenshire *cynghanedd* with Mr Len Muncer (harp), Mr Gilbert Parkhouse (Velindre bagpipes), Mr Don Shepherd (spoons), and Mr Tony Cordle (mezzo-soprano).

He had lunched well.

The Dee salmon poached in goats' milk and Preseli fennel had been outstanding.

The wines had made sweet and languid music on his palate. He had particularly revelled in a vintage Château Solanky and the arrogant, full-bodied elegance of the Niersteiner Guter Majid Khan.

He was in a benign mood.

At that very moment he had at his disposal two livings, both of which were sinecures in their different manners.

One was the rectorship of St Wilfred, the blessed Rhodes.

The other was editor-in-chief of the *Sunday Telegraph*.

In the full flood of his post-prandial beneficence, he decided that he would offer these livings to the first person he saw on leaving the pavilion.

Thankfully, he did not notice Miss Dorothy Squires slinking out of the Gareth Edwards portable temperance tea rooms.

Instead his gaze fell upon the minute figure of Mole-Drably scurrying to the changing room to don his umpire's garb.

'You!' he bellowed in the manner with which he customarily addressed recalcitrant junior sub-editors and insubordinate captains of England.

Mole-Drably froze in his tracks.

Was it God who had spoken to him?

Had the creator of Heaven and Earth and E.R.Dexter and all the goodnesses thereof chosen to address him in that icy wilderness on the North Wales coast?

Once more he heard those ringing, celestial tones:

'You! Shortarse!'

Scarcely daring to breathe, he turned.

He saw an impressive figure with a leonine mane of snow-white hair and an imperious jut to the jaw.

Yes, it *was* God.

And he was wearing MCC suspenders.

He flung himself on his knees.

And there and then he was granted the benefice of St Wilfred, the Blessed Rhodes.

With what joy he scurried home and flung away the impedimenta of his office as chaplain-general to Sealink – the self-righting dog collar, the inflatable font with snorkel attachment and the bell-bottom cassock.

With what ecstacy he strode down the gravelled driveway of the vicarage of St Wilfred, the Blessed Rhodes, with its rambling roses, its *Leylandi Wilsonia* and its *Erica Sutcliffia*.

And there for the past ten years he has ministered to his flocks with gentleness and humility.

With what tender nostalgia he recounts the highlights of that past decade – his part in the ordination into the BBC of the Rev. F. S. Trueman, his influence on the conversion of Saint Raymond D'Illingworth from his 'Leicester heresy' and his sympathetic intervention during the distressing circumstances surrounding the defrocking of Canon Close.

To my mind, however, it is his sermons which have most distinguished his ministry, and it is with great pride that I reprint the sermon he gave during my most recent visit to his church.

'The text of my sermon today is taken from the following:

"And, behold, Ron Saggers did tour England with the 1948 Australians and, lo, not a single Test did he play in."

'Isn't there a lesson there for all of us?

'The selfless devotion to duty; the debasement of self-interest to the greater good of the team.

'Life is like a cricket tour, isn't it?

'Some of us reach the eminence of an Ernie Toshak.

'Some of us achieve the moderate success of a Doug Ring.

'But for most of us life is a condition of the perpetual Ron Saggers, constant toilers in obscurity, loyal lieutenants to 'the top brass', humble participants in an endless match against Minor Counties on a bleak September afternoon in Jesmond.

'I never met Ron Saggers myself.

'If, however, my Lord and Maker, the creator of E. R. Dexter, Heaven and Earth in that order, were to grant me such joy, I should grasp him by the hand, shake it firmly and say in the manner to which he and his compatriots are accustomed:

'"Good on you, sport. Give my regards to the sheila and let's crack a tube of the old Swans."

'What do I mean by 'a tube of the old Swans'?

'I mean, don't I, that rounded metal object which contains a particularly powerful and nauseous beverage drunk in enormous quantities by our Antipodean cousins and used extensively throughout our great Commonwealth of nations for the dispersal of mosquitoes and the scouring of lavatory pans.

'Life is like a tube of Swans, isn't it?

'For most of us it is a powerful brew, which, if taken in excessive quantities, induces premature baldness and the growth of unwanted hair on the palms of our hands.

'But need we take life in excessive quantities?

'Is there no reason why we should not take it in moderation?

'Let us take a lesson from the cricket field.

'It is the fast bowler, isn't it, who takes all the glory and all the honour.

'But it is the slow bowler, weaving his subtle spells, who ultimately is still playing with distinction and enjoyment long after the fast bowler has "hung up his boots".

'Is it not significant that it was a slow bowler, Mr Eric Hollies, who accounted for the wicket of the great Sir Donald Bradman, in the last Test match he ever played in this country?

'And is there not an example there for all of us?

'If we want to get the most out of life, let us flex our spinning fingers constantly, let us practise diligently in the nets of godliness and always bowl to a good length on the pitch of holiness and never, never play with dirty flannels or dispute the umpire's decision.

'What do I mean by "Umpire's decision"?

'I mean, don't I, those few seconds after the bowler has appealed against the batsman, and we await in a limbo of apprehension as to whether the white-coated gent with the sweaters strung round his waist will raise a forefinger denoting that the batsman is out or turn on his heel shaking his head and muttering:

'"Piss off, you barmy chuff."

'I am reminded here of that great and saintly Lancashire cricketer, Mr Winston Place, who on retiring from the first-class game took up umpiring.

'He resigned from his position, however, because such was his goodness and his benevolence, he could not bear to give people out.

'God is rather like Winston Place, although I suspect

he does not have ginger hair and is not so accomplished a late cutter.

'He doesn't like giving us "out".

'And, of course, if we play a straight bat in the game of life, always move our body into the line of the ball and never flash outside the off stump, there is no reason why God should ever give us "out" until the time comes at the end of the day when the heavenly scorer nods in his drowsy hut and the celestial barmaid places the seraphic tea towels over the ethereal beer pumps, and He declares our "innings closed".

'Let us, therefore, resolve to put on the cricket togs of life with hope and with joy and with love.

'With radiance and gladsomeness in our hearts let us buckle on our pads, shake the dandruff out of our caps, wipe the egg stains off our sweaters and adjust our abdominal protectors.

'What do I mean by "abdominal protectors"?

'I mean, don't I, that device made in former times of metal and canvas and now these days manufactured from reinforced plastic, which men strap over their most private parts to protect them from life's shooters, yorkers and fast full tosses.

'Dear friends, let the love of God be your abdominal protector.

'Let His mercy and His unbounding wisdom be your thigh pad and your lightweight helmet.

'Let His compassion and His clemency for the basest of sinner be your Gunn and Moore jock strap.

'Dear friends, if you want the best out of life, always shop at God's.

'Thank you.

'Next week my text will be:
'"And, lo, Gordon Garlick did smite mighty sixes for Lancashire and then of a sudden was he transferred to Northamptonshire".'

I find that oddly comforting, don't you?

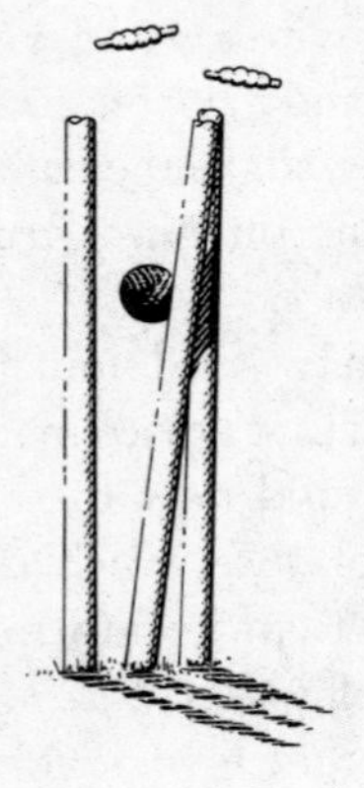

6
The Lady Wife

The lady wife, like most members of her sex (which is female), has an inordinate number of birthdays.

As she grows older these undoubtedly increase in frequency.

Indeed I am of the opinion that she is now celebrating as many as one per annum.

This year, I suppose, she will have a birthday on the Saturday of the Lords Test.

She usually does.

And as always when she informs me of the impending approach of this frightful event, I shall look at her, and I shall think to myself – why?

Why, why, why?

Why on earth did I ever marry her?

Certainly there was a physical attraction. That I cannot deny.

I remember to this day the surge of emotion that coursed through my veins when I first caught sight of her.

The rose garden at dear old Castle Arlott slumbering with honey-laden bees.

The gentle summer breeze lisping through the timid tracery of the delicate Frindall tree.

The Benaud bush aflame in scarlet bloom. The phlox Lakeriensis flowering hazily lazily benignly blue.

And into my view she glided; a tall, slim, sylphlike figure in purest white.

My heart missed a beat.

The sap rose in my loins.

Dear God, she was the spitting image of Herbert Sutcliffe.

It was love at first sight.

Call it the impetuosity of youth if you will, but remember I had been out of the country for many years, serving my King and country in some of the remotest and most primitive outposts of his Empire.

I had not seen a first-class county cricketer for seven years.

I was desperate.

I was bewitched.

I was overwhelmed.

We married that autumn in the exquisite little Saxon church at Witney Scrotum, and as we walked down the aisle arm in arm embarking upon a career of conjugal concomitance I felt for all the world as Percy Holmes must have felt walking out to open the innings for Yorkshire at five past six on a grey, chill September evening at Trent Bridge with Harold Larwood glowering and snarling in the gloom at the Radcliffe Road end.

Our marriage, I am bound to say, has not been all gloom and misery. There have been moments of radiant happiness and unrestrained joy, when it seems that the earth has moved and the heavenly choirs have burst into anthems of passion, and in the soft afterglow I have turned to my wife and said:

'Right, it's your go now. But remember – you mustn't move your legs.'

She always was a duffer at french cricket.

There have been moments, too, when the chores of nuptial incumbency have been enlightened by occasions of solemn levity.

In this context I recall with particular pleasure an afternoon at Cheltenham.

My wife as she approached her prime grew to look more and more like that great Gloucestershire all-rounder, T. W. Goddard.

It was a source of much pride and satisfaction to me, none more so than on that sun-dappled post-prandial session at the Cheltenham Festival, when we were sitting with friends idly nibbling chilled Zubes and supping our mulled Château Dipper.

Our peace and serenity was rudely disturbed when the Gloucestershire skipper, Mr B. O. Allen, strode up to us angrily, pointed an accusatory finger at the lady wife and said in a most hectoring manner:

'Goddard, what in the name of blitheration are you doing there sitting dressed in women's togs? Get yourself off to the dressing room this instant.'

This the lady wife did.

And at the end of the day she had the satisfaction of returning home having taken seven Leicestershire wickets at a cost of a mere seventeen runs.

But moments such as these have been rare indeed in our marriage.

How many nights have I lain awake in bed with soft owls hooting and whiskers of rain snarling at the window pane, and I have raised myself on one arm and looked down at the slumbering form of the lady wife and I have thought to myself:

'My God, I wish you were someone else.'

Admit it, dear friends.

I am not alone in these thoughts.

How many of you while engaged in the most intimate activity in which man and wife can be involved have closed your eyes and thought to yourself at the moment of delivery – by jingo, I wish you were the Nawab of Pataudi.

How many of you have not craved for the warm, passionate propinquity of a Fred Rumsey or the soft, whispered blandishments of a David Bairstow?

Certainly with me it is the 'physical' side of things which have proved most irksome in my marriage.

I am convinced, for example, that it was those bi-monthly Friday night sessions with the light out which were the ultimate cause of a serious weakness in my spinning finger and an inability to achieve a consistent full length.

Nothing will dissuade me from the view that had I not been married to the lady wife, I should have opened the innings for England, captained the Gentlemen against the Players and in the fullness of time achieved the greatest honour any cricketer can attain to – being granted an audience of Mr E. R. Dexter.

Friends tell me that circumstances might have been different had the lady wife and I had issue.

Who can say?

Was Joe Hardstaff, senior, a happier man for having produced Joe Hardstaff, junior?

What gave Mr and Mrs Gibbs more satisfaction – producing one of the finest off-spinners the world has ever known or inventing toothpaste?

Would it have been a consolation to Mr Neville Chamberlain in the darkest days after Munich to know that one day his son, 'Tosh', would play outside left for Fulham?

I think not.

I am reminded of a dear and precious friend of mine, who produced a family of truly extravagant proportions.

I met him in the Long Room at Lords shortly after the birth of yet another of his progeny.

His mien was downcast. His face was bleak.

'Well?' I said. 'What is it this time?'

He looked at me silently for a moment.

And then he muttered savagely:

'Another bloody leg spinner.'

I am bound to confess in fairness, however, that in certain matters of a domestic nature the lady wife has been of help to me.

It was her handiwork with needle and thread which on many occasions has saved me from the distress of having to take a well-loved jock strap to the vet to be put down.

Her dexterity on the fretwork machine saved me from the considerable expense of replacing a sight-screen, groundsman's hut and portable ablutions facility destroyed under circumstances which even now I find too painful to recall.

No, weighing the pros and cons of our marriage in the balance, it is evident to me that but for the frequency of her birthdays, the lady wife might have become a reasonably tolerant companion.

I will go further.

It is not the birthdays *per se* which have caused me such discomfort, it is the necessity of purchasing presents which I have found so damnable.

No sooner has the wretched thing been handed over at the breakfast table than one is compelled to enter once more the nauseous and time-consuming palaver of thinking of a suitable gift for the next birthday.

It would not be irksome if the lady wife were to show even a modicum of gratitude for my offering.

'Oh, crumbs, not another one?' is her customary reaction. 'Why can't you think of something original for a change?'

Well, what she fails to appreciate is that the shop at Lords does not have an inexhaustible supply of novelties.

Dear God, she already has three different versions of the Gubby Allen toilet bag, and I simply refuse to pay out good money in purchasing yet aother Alec Bedser pyjama case.

Stubbornly and steadfastly the lady wife refuses to

believe that the Ken Higgs autograph negligees and the gift-wrapped bottles of Eau de Washbrook are invariably snapped up by the MCC committee members long before the shop opens for its summer season.

How different it would all be if my wife were not to have birthdays.

How different indeed it would be if no one were to have birthdays, if life were to become a 'timeless test', if we were to be spared the death and decay which comes to all from the relentless passing of the years.

Would the world not be a better place today if Jack Hobbs were still wielding his silken willow, our city streets still rang to the echoes of carthorse hooves clopping on preening cobbles, and Mr 'Stainless' Stephen still tickled our chuckle muscles on our faithful cat's whisker?

Would not life be richer today if Spofforth and 'W. G.' were still engaged in mortal combat and the endless sunshine of 'The Golden Age' lit up in its radiance the bleakness and despair of this age of cold war, nancy boys and aluminium bats?

But no, dear friends, these are but the pipedreams of an old man.

Let us be happy with what we have.

I look now with surprising affection on the lady wife as she sits in our oak-timbered drawing room, her needles flashing in the flames of the log fire as she knits yet another set of nets for Mr Alf Gover's indoor cricket school.

And I think to myself – grow old in your own time, my dear.

Let the silver mingle with the gold.

Let us give succour and comfort to each other as our innings draws inexorably to its close.

But when you next have a birthday, for pity's sake let it be on the second day of Minor Counties versus Indian Tourists.

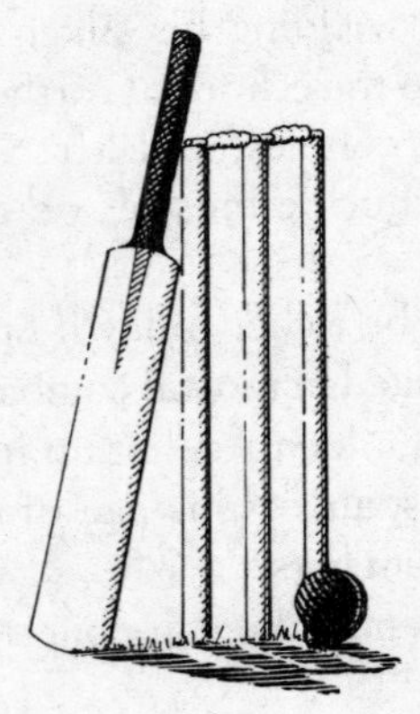

7
The Groundsman's Horse

During the course of a long and happy life one emotion has remained in my heart unfailingly and unflinchingly in the face of all the dangers and horrors that Mother Nature could throw at me – hurricane, typhoon, earthquake, war, famine, the cricket reports of Mr Tony Lewis.

The emotion is this:

An undying love for all our 'dumb friends'.

Thus it is that over the years I have cast my vote loyally and consistently for the Conservative and Unionist Party.

Thus it is that I send anonymously a bag of carrots each week to the BBC for the personal consumption of

Mr Raymond Brooks-Ward.

Thus it is, too, that I have steadfastly maintained my membership of The Tiger Tim Appreciation Society and been unstinting in my admiration for that great and noble statesman, philosopher, Olympic athlete and England opening bat, wicket-keeper and fast bowler, Lord Mountbatman of Burma.

It is the mention of Burma which reminds me of an episode in my life pertaining to our 'dumb friends', which even now many, many years later brings a glow of pride and feelings of the deepest satisfaction.

I was in Burma in the company of my father, who at the time was acting as adviser to the colonial administration during a particularly tricky outbreak of sight-screen desecration among the hill tribes of the Shan Plateau.

They were worrying times.

The Shans were seeking to impose their own version of the lbw rule on the loyal population of the towns and villages, and there were dark reports of the harassment of umpires and baggage masters in inaccessible valleys, over which MCC had only the most tenuous of influence.

My father, however, was a sanguine man.

Years of service in the farthest outposts of the British Empire had taught him that only the basest of savages, the most primitive of barbarians would fail to respond to the blandishments of a peace party of I Zingari mercenaries, who would play a ceremonial limited-over match with the dissidents and distribute to the masses free supplies of bakelite statuettes of Mr E.R. Dexter.

The efficacy of his philosophy had been proved time

and time again in the harsh experience of 'action in the field'.

Indeed at that time the only remaining pocket of resistance to MCC rule in the whole of the British Empire existed in remote islands of the Cocos group and certain recalcitrant city states in the West Riding of Yorkshire.

So it was that as we strolled through that Burmese town basking in the full and gentle bloom of a simpering spring afternoon there was a confident lilt to my father's tread and the faintest whisper of a smile upon his face.

He was happily recounting to me stories of early days spent on active service with The Royal Burma Frontier Scouts ('Plum' Warner's Own) when of a sudden he stopped dead in his tracks

His eyes widened.

His lower lip sagged.

And he exclaimed:

'Good God, laddie, look at that.'

I followed the direction of the pointing forearm.

And there a most singular sight struck my youthful eyes.

A broken-backed nag, head bowed, ribs protruding through scabrous flesh, matted fetlocks slouching through tropic dust, was plodding wearily down the centre of the pockmarked highway.

At its head was an emaciated figure in scarecrow rags, his bare feet blistered and scarred, his unkempt beard straggling over a hollow, naked chest and his sunken cheeks engrimed by the dust and dirt of years of neglect.

My father forthwith grasped my hand firmly and, striding purposefully across the street, placed himself forcefully in front of the horse and man.

'Whoa!' he bellowed.

Horse and man stopped, although neither raised its head.

'It isn't? It can't be,' said my father, and slowly and carefully he encircled the two wretched figures, his eyes narrowed, his brow furrowed.

Then he exclaimed:

'By jingo, it is. It's the groundsman's horse from Swanton St George.'

The effect of my father's words on the horse's attendant was remarkable to behold.

A choked gurgle came to his throat.

His bloodshot eyes rolled in their deep black sockets.

His knees began to tremble and suddenly he collapsed to the ground in a dead swoon.

I moved forward, but my father drew me back.

'Leave him be,' he shouted.

I froze in my tracks.

Silence.

My father clicked his tongue and swatted his thigh with the quarter-sized, bullet-scarred Strutt and Parker cricket bat he carried with him everywhere as protection against mosquitoes and my beloved mother's bad temper.

He was motionless for what seemed to me an eternity (almost as long as an innings by Mr Trevor Bailey, I was to think much later).

Then, wrinkling his nose, he extended his right leg and with the toe of his boot turned over the poor wretch who was still lying on the ground in the deepest of faints.

I gasped.

It was a white man.

My father grunted to himself with evident satisfaction.

Then he turned his attention to the pitiful nag which stood by his side, swatting its emaciated rump with a threadbare tail, vainly trying to keep at bay the attentions of the legions of flies which swarmed about its various orifices in a cloying, buzzing black mass like a clutch of animated eccles cakes.

My father nodded.

'Yes, by thunderation, it is the groundsman's horse,' he said, 'And I shall prove it to you forthwith.'

And with that he threw back his head and roared in a stentorian voice:

'Heavy roller!'

The effect was instantaneous.

The horse laid its ears flat against its skull, drew back its lips to reveal a set of yellowing and splintered teeth, and quite without warning lowered its head, lashed out with its back feet and set off at a canter down the dusty road, bucking and whinnying for all the world like Mr Ian Chappell appealing for lbw against Miss Rachel Heyhoe-Flint.

My father nodded again.

'That proves it conclusively,' he said. 'It always was shy of hard work with the roller.'

The horse did not travel far.

Such was the parlous nature of its condition that after twenty yards it ceased its mad flight and stood in the shade of a Robertson-Glasgow tree, wheezing and panting, its flanks shaking uncontrollably.

My father arranged for both horse and attendant to

be transported to our bungalow.

There in the stables in the shade of the giant Johnstonian oaks and the brooding Fingleton palms they were fed and watered and bedded down for the night in warm, clean hay.

It took a week for both to recover, and then my father was to learn from the groundsman (for thus was the identity of the poor wretch who had collapsed before his feet) the true story of their banishment to a land so different from the lush greensward and billowing beeches of their native Swanton St George.

Apparently the groundsman's horse had long been a feared institution at the village cricket team.

A fierce, uncontrollable brute, it obeyed only the commands of the groundsman, Festering, a sly and sullen lout of a man with a nose like a wicket-keeper's thumb.

It was allowed to graze unhindered on the village cricket pitch.

Such was its ill temper and ferocity that its presence was not removed even during the progress of matches.

No one dared approach it save for the groundsman, and thus a local rule was established: if the ball hit the horse, wheresoever it was standing, a four was awarded.

Most visiting teams were prepared to accept this condition, and all went well until the arrival of an Australian touring team, the Marsupials.

The Antipodean wanderers were skippered by Warren Croaker, who was later to achieve cricketing immortality by beating to death an umpire, with whose decision he disagreed (a practice much favoured by later generations of Australian Test cricketers).

Croaker was tried, convicted and sentenced to be executed by firing squad.

Dressed in flannels, pads and typical 'baggy' cap he was bound to the sight-screen at the Adelaide Oval and shot by a detachment of The Third Battalion Sam Loxton Dragoons.

His last words as he lay dying were reported to have been:

'Thank God, I was wearing my box.'

However, I digress.

Back to the match, Swanton St George versus The Marsupials.

The visitors from 'Down Under' took first knock and quickly amassed the staggering total of 239.

Swanton St George commenced their innings and were soon in 'the deepest trouble' at thirty-four for eight.

Certain defeat stared them in the face (to use the immortal and memorable words of that undisputed doyen of cricket writers, Mr E. R. Dexter).

It was at this moment that the groundsman, Festering, appeared at the wicket.

At once the wheels of the score-box began to whirr as, to use the expression of our Antipodean cousins from across the seas, the 'curator' struck four after four after four off his opponents' bowling.

But one thing was strikingly obvious – each of his fours was gained by the ball's hitting the grazing horse.

Slowly but surely the Swanton St George total approached the forbidding total set by their guests, the descendants of convicts, murderers and de-frocked members of MCC.

The 200 was reached when a ball smitten by Festering struck the horse a sickening blow on the left off paston.

The 220 was reached by the ball's hitting the heedless nag a resounding smack on a rump, the size of which was only exceeded many years later by the posterior portions of Mr M. C. Cowdrey.

It was then that (to borrow once more the sublime prose of Mr E. R. Dexter) 'excitement reached fever pitch'.

One over to go. Fifteen runs required.

Partnering Festering was the padre of the village, the Rev. Marchling-Thumper, who was later to become private chaplain to *The Sporting Chronicle*.

He was facing the bowling of the Australian skipper, Croaker.

The first delivery he received struck him a blistering blow in the ribcage.

'Run, you sod,' bellowed Festering.

The clerical gent scampered breathlessly to the bowler's end, glowering darkly at Festering, whose ill-chosen words had so offended his frail and delicate spirit.

One run gained. Fourteen to go.

It was then that spectators noticed a most singular occurrence – the groundsman's horse was approaching nearer and nearer to the wicket.

More singular still, it was actually beginning to move in the direction of each ball struck by Festering.

One four.

Two fours.

A wild swipe that did not connect.

A two, when a 'Chinese drive' flashed over first slip.

One ball to go. Four runs needed for victory.

Croaker polished the ball on his gin-stained flannels, glowering the while out of the corner of his eyes at the groundsman's horse.

He bowled.

Festering struck out.

The ball travelled no more than five feet on the off side.

The Australians cried out jubilantly.

Surely no more than a single could be obtained from the stroke?

But no.

The groundsman's horse threw back its head, whinnied and galloping like a dervish through the crowded off-side field, butted the Australian backward point just as he was about to pounce on the ball.

The Antipodean fell to the ground, shattering his hip flask beyond redemption.

The horse with a wicked grin of triumph bent down and gently nuzzled the ball towards the umpire.

'Four,' yelled Festering. 'The ball touched the horse. We've won.'

There are no words to do justice to the uproar that followed.

Not even the combined efforts of the pens of Mr Tony Lewis, Mr E. R. Dexter and 'the Proust of cricket literature', Mr Robin Marlar, could bring it to life on the printed page.

Accusation was followed by counter-accusation.

Wild imprecations filled the gentle English country air.

Such was the vileness of the Australian oaths that the bells in the church belfry were shattered to smithereens, and the treasured statue of the Blessed St Tony Greig of the Sorrows was split from cravat to money belt.

Peace was only restored when the Rev. Marchling-Thumper, who had taken refuge in the communal cricket bag, emerged from his hiding place white and trembling and, in a sacerdotal voice reminiscent of the dulcet tones of Mr Bill Alley at his most pious, shouted:

'Stop. Stop, I beg you.'

The clerical gent pointed a wavering forefinger at the groundsman, Festering, who was placidly feeding to his horse liberal quantities of Grannie Sinfield's Home-Made Gloucester Fudge.

'There is your culprit,' said the cricketing prelate.

Instantly Festering was surrounded by players from both sides.

His arms were twisted, his ribs were pummelled and he was forced to confess.

His plot was simple, effective and fiendish – he had trained his horse to run after balls hit by him and allow them to strike its body.

Shame. Disgrace.

The skipper of the village team apologized profusely to Croaker.

The provision of eight firkins of prime Rae and Stollmeyer dark English ale and seventeen local virgins was sufficient to assuage him.

The apologies were accepted.

And thus it was that Festering and his horse were banished in ignominy to far-off Burma.

And as they plodded up the gangplank to the steamer which was to take them from Southampton to Rangoon, a voice addressed to Festering piped up from the back of the crowd.

'Run, you sod,' it said.

The voice belonged to the Rev. Marchling-Thumper.

My father listened to the story with tears in his eyes.

'You have suffered enough,' he said to Festering. 'Now I shall give you peace. Now I shall lead you to a land where everything you desire will be granted to you.'

Within the week he had taken the groundsman and his horse to the rebellious regions of the Shan plateau.

The effect was amazing.

The Shan tribesmen, primitive and innocent as they were, had never in the whole of their lives seen such a creature.

They threw down their arms, abandoned their lbw mutiny, and within weeks had settled down to a life of peace and obedience.

Indeed such was their amazement at this strange creature which had come to their midst from lands thousands of miles across the oceans that they deified it immediately.

And to this day the creature is to be seen stuffed and standing in a place of honour in the chief township of the Shan plateau.

Although what happened to the groundsman's horse is still unknown.

8
Mendip-Hughes

There is an old adage unique to this beloved 'summer game' of ours: 'the hour findeth the man'.

How true.

How often have cricketers been plucked from obscurity, thrown into the harsh spotlight of fame and notoriety and thus 'found' themselves and emblazened their names gloriously and permanently in the panoply of cricket's hall of fame?

We recall the immortal Fuller Pilch, hoisted from the vast brooding fastness of Norfolk to become one of the towering legendary figures of his age.

We think of the great Frank Tyson, dragged from the mediocrity of county cricket to become 'the scourge' of

Australian batsmen with the ferocity of his fast bowling.

We think of David Steele, plucked from obscurity of leadership of the Liberal Party to don the noble sweater of England and face unflinchingly the might of Lilley and Thompson.

And we think, too, of Geoff Boycott, plucked from the vast brooding fastness, the mediocrity and the obscurity of a Michael Parkinson chat show to become one of the greatest accumulators of runs known to the modern game.

Such a man was the one-legged Somerset off-spinner, Mendip-Hughes.

Let me state my attitude to him without prevarication:

It is my firm opinion that he was the finest uniped never to represent his country at Test match level.

I believe, moreover, that it was only prejudice of the basest sort which kept from him the representative honours given to men, the number of whose appendages may have been superior, but the number of whose talents was most definitely inferior.

I have no time for prejudice of any sort.

Mendip-Hughes should have been selected solely on his merits as an off-spinner.

He was not a nigger.

He was not an oily Italian, a foul-smelling Argentinian or a typical cowardly, wife-beating, dishonest, hysterical, garlic-munching Frenchman.

There was no excuse whatsoever for the selectors' failure to grant him the England cap he so richly deserved.

And so I feel it is high time he was given his 'just desserts'.

With that in mind I have composed the following short monograph.

It is generally assumed by historians of the 'summer game' that Mendip-Hughes lost his left leg during the first German offensive on the Somme in 1915.

This is not the case.

At the time in question Mendip-Hughes would have been approaching his sixth birthday, and, despite considerable research through the military archives, I have found no evidence to suggest that the British Army employed in its front line soldiers of such tender years.

No.

Let us scotch that particular rumour here and now.

Let us instead hoist our flag unashamedly to the assertion that the missing left leg, with which we now deal, met its demise in a piano accident at Crewkerne.

Mendip-Hughes himself was always most reticent in discussing the exact nature of the incident.

Who shall blame him?

There is a regrettable tendency these days for what I call 'Public Nosey Parkering'.

Fed by the unceasing efforts of journalists, broadcasters and similar scum, the British public has developed an insatiable appetite for tittle-tattle of the most trivial nature concerning people who for one reason or the other happen to be 'in the limelight'.

What possible interest can it be to know that E. W. Swanton wears maroon corduroy underpants and has in his study the complete collection of the records of Billy J. Kramer and the Dakotas?

Is the world a better place for knowing that despite all the evidence to the contrary Mr Robin Marlar is a thoroughly nice man?

Are we uplifted in soul and spirit by the knowledge that, despite his constant protestations, Mr Ned Sherrin did indeed once play rugby league football for Rochdale Hornets? – the match in which Miss Caryl Brahms was sent 'for an early bath' for butting an opponent.

No, let us draw a veil over Mendip-Hughes's unfortunate accident and say nothing about his mother's appalling carelessness in keeping a loaded Japanese blunderbuss in the piano stool and a Snoad and Hazelhurst Patent Poachers' Anti-Personnel Trap under the lid of the piano.

Let us concentrate on the influences which shaped the future distinguished career of Mendip-Hughes.

From the outset he was determined that regardless of his pedicular deficiency he would be 'Like all the other chaps'.

This indeed he was.

Like all boys of his age and background he became an accomplished player of the banjole, an expert in the early works of Krafft-Ebing, a most proficient translator into English of the writings of Mr E. W. Swanton, and winner in 1930 of the world's first one-legged ping-pong championship when he beat the Dane, Lars Erik Mortensen, 21-7 in the final set.

A brilliant career in diplomacy, banking, the university or wholesale greengrocery seemed assured to him.

Then came the untimely and catastrophic collapse of the family fortunes in 1931.

The painful details of this incident are best left covered in the mists of time.

What right have we to shake off the dust of faded memory and expose once more to public gaze the abject humiliation of Mendip-Hughes *père* with the collapse of his Surinam Steam Laundry Company and the subsequent allegations of forged banknotes, bribery, black magic and gross sexual impropriety?

That is voyeurism of 'the worst sort' and is best left to those pedlars of filth and gossip, whose livings are earned feasting on the carrion of others' misfortunes.

Let us return to poor Mendip-Hughes, penniless, without prospects and cast adrift with the MCC Cricketing Freaks, which toured the world in 1933.

The party was led by Mr M. P. Bradwell-Jackson, the short-sighted Oxfordshire wicket-keeper, who was later to achieve cricketing immortality in 1956 by proposing marriage to Mr K. D. 'Slasher' Mackay of Queensland and Australia during tea interval at the Cheltenham Festival.

The tour was an outstanding success.

There were notable victories over a Turkish Transvestites Eleven, a Peruvian Onanists Select, and a most exciting tied match with the Bondage and Nude Bicycling Gymkhana of Bombay.

For Mendip-Hughes, however, the tour meant nothing but misery and despair and frustration.

He was constantly no-balled in Tibet.

He had trouble with his run up in Brazzaville.

His cricket bag was eaten by spectators in Borneo.

It was not until the final match of the tour, a three-day contest against Twelve Amputees of Arabia, that a chink of light appeared in the tunnel of gloom and darkness.

Mendip-Hughes was 'spotted' by a member of the committee of the Somerset County Cricket Club who, as luck would have it, was serving a brief spell as Director General Royal Ablutions to the Sultan of Oman.

This perspicacious gentleman immediately telegraphed Taunton, and within the month Mendip-Hughes had joined the county of the winged dragon to embark upon a career that was as dazzling as it was brief.

There is no need for me to dwell on his deeds on the cricket fields.

No one who saw him is ever likely to forget that distinctive bound and hop to the wicket, that jack-in-the-box spring as he released the ball, that strangled, tortured cry as he leapt one-legged high into the air to appeal to the umpire.

Let us rather concentrate on his subsequent career off the field, over which totally unjustifiable clouds of suspicion and calumny have been cast.

Let us destroy once and for all the vile rumour that Mendip-Hughes's sudden disappearance from the cricket scene in August 1936 was the result of 'an incident' with the groundsman's horse at Wells.

One has only to read that sadly neglected volume, *The Pensées of Horace Hazell*, to be given 'the true story'.

Suffice it to say that even at the time I myself was convinced that the horse's undoubted distress had more to do with its purloining and subsequent consumption of Harold Gimblett's jock strap than any misdemeanour on the part of Mendip-Hughes.

The reasons for the sudden retirement of Mendip-Hughes are more fascinating and compelling than that.

For the first time, freed from the constrictions of the Official Secrets Act, I can reveal that on that fateful day at Wells Mendip-Hughes was summoned to 'higher things'.

He was called to the service of King and country to establish in M15 its first Cricket Section.

For many months previously secret service chiefs and their political masters had been eyeing the activities of Nazi Germany and Fascist Italy with considerable suspicion.

It was, I believe, the uniform opinion of those august gentlemen that Herr Hitler and Signor Mussolini could only be described as stinkers and out-and-out rotters.

This opinion was born out many years later by Germany's vile and wanton destruction of the cricket pavilion at Old Trafford, and the totally unprovoked attack by incendiary bombs and parachute aerial mines on the Farmer White Home for Retired Leg Spinners at Keating St Rodda.

Accordingly they conceived the daring and novel notion that, if clandestine relationships could be established in Germany and Italy with people of a cricketing bent, a popular uprising could be engendered which would sweep away forever the odious dictatorships and restore in their place a free society, in which the jack boot would be replaced by the cricket boot and the rhino whip would give way to the Gunn and Moore three-springer.

It was not for want of industry or courage that Mendip-Hughes failed to bring their plans to fulfilment.

Despite a natural and totally justifiable dislike of his colleagues in M15, a loathesome collection of nancy boys and ladies with loud voices and hairy chests, Mendip-Hughes threw himself into his new job with enthusiasm and a reckless disregard for his own safety.

It is not generally known that Mendip-Hughes narrowly escaped death in 1938 when he was arrested in Berlin and charged with the illegal distribution of cricket balls, which he had brought into the country concealed in the false bottom of a cricket bag.

Few people, I am certain, are aware that Mendip-Hughes only narrowly failed to persuade Count Ciano to bring a representative eleven of his black shirts to play Mr H. D. G. Leweson-Gower's Eleven at the Scarborough Festival of 1939.

In the same year Mendip-Hughes achieved the triumph of inducing Reichsmarschall Hermann Goering and his wife to attend the Saturday of the Lords Test.

No blame can be attached to him for the fact that when the time came there were no tickets available, and the obese Hum and his odious spouse were compelled to spend the afternoon at Buckingham Palace playing three-card brag with Queen Mary and Princess Alice of Athlone.

One can only conjecture sadly about how different the fate of the world would have been, had this and other enterprises been granted with success.

Alas, it was not to be.

Neither was Mendip-Hughes to be granted further opportunity to exercise his talents, for war was declared shortly after Goering's return to his native heath and our hero was straightway plunged into the nefarious world of intrigue and espionage.

Very few details remain concerning the termination of his career with M15.

We do know that during the war he made several dangerous and arduous missions to occupied Europe.

We know that on his last mission he was parachuted into Vichy France early in the spring of 1943.

From this he did not return.

No one is sure of the exact nature of his fate. However, one interesting fact has recently come to light.

There has been discovered a small and remote village in the heart of the Auvergne, in which the men to this very day play cricket.

Even more fascinating is the fact that they play cricket on one leg.

It would be comforting to think that this is the legacy Mendip-Hughes left to posterity, although it must be pointed out that Mendip-Hughes played cricket on his right leg, while the men of the Auvergne play on their left leg.

Let us be charitable and state that this is yet another example of the entrenched Gallic obstinacy when faced with the noble culture and moral values of England.

9
Cricketers' Cook Book

In my experience, cricketers and all those associated with our beloved 'summer game' are without exception outstanding trenchermen.

I recall Nuttall, the Lancashire professional, who once ate half a carthorse during the luncheon adjournment in a match against Leicestershire.

He claimed he would have eaten the whole of the horse, had the bridle not stuck in his teeth.

I remember Sumpter, a drinking man of heroic proportions who once drank ten quarts of claret and a can of linseed oil before going out to bat against Gentlemen of Ulster (they could only find five, incidentally).

He is the only man in history as having been given out:

'Drunk hit wicket and umpire.'

With this in mind I have collected a few favourite recipes of cricketers both famous and humble, and these I present for your delectation and edification.

Alec Bedser's Fancy

Alec Bedser writes:

'I like incredibly boring food.

'And so does my brother.

'I like sausages and chips. I think this is the most incredibly boring food I know.

'And so does my brother.

'When you are making sausages and chips, the first thing to do is to buy the ingredients.

'This is quite easy.

'First of all you go to the butcher's with your brother, and you say:

' "A pound of sausages, please."

'The butcher will probably say:

' "Certainly, sir, what sort do you require?"

'You answer:

' "Pork, please."

'The butcher will in all likelihood then reply:

' "Can't I tempt you with the beef, sir? They are highly recommended."

'You reply:

' "Pork, please."

'His next tack will be to say:

' "What about the herb sausages, sir?"

'You reply:

' "Pork, please."

'If he should then go on to say:

' "The tomato-flavoured are very delicious, sir."

'You reply:

' "Pork, please."

'Next you go to the greengrocer's.

'And so does your brother.

'You say to the greengrocer:

' "Five pounds of potatoes, please."

'The greengrocer will in all probability say:

' "Certainly, sir. What variety do you require – King Edwards, Lincolnshire red, waxy whites, Pentland Squire or Pembrokeshire new?"

'You reply:

' "I don't give a shit."

'After this you go home.

'And so does your brother.

'Now it gets even more incredibly boring.

'You have to cook it.

'Usually I don't bother.

'I let my brother do it.'

My dear, dear friend, Robert Carrier, is not only a noted gourmet and epicure, he is also something of a cricket fanatic.

What happy memories I have of enchanting week-ends spent at his bewitching country home.

All those lovely young men arrayed in flannels and silk shirts of purest white disporting themselves on the cricket field, while dear Bob tirelessly and selflessly worked in the kitchen chopping up the pickled onions for the post-match hot-pot supper.

What bliss.

On my last visit to his home he set before me a magnificent display of some of his favourite cakes and puddings.

This is my report on them:

Arlott Cake. A rich, fruity concoction. Aromatic and deeply satisfying to the soul. A cake to linger over on long, brooding winter evenings. A cake to eat with vintage port. Scrumptious.

Swanton Pudding. A heavy, suet-based confectionary which I found intimidating and indigestible. It turned the custard lumpy.

Keating Krackle. A delicious, spicey biscuit. A little too eager to please, perhaps, but full of subtlety and delicate flavour. Delicious accompaniment to the incomparable Cook and Wells Gloucester country cider.

Auntie Lewis's Welsh Tart. An over-fussy dessert. Looks all right on the outside, but its flavour is inconsequential and its texture is irritatingly bland.

Jonner's Jam Sandwich. A jolly cake full of fun and hearty flavour. Marvellous for tuck boxes and midnight feasts in the dorm.

Marlar Melting Moments. Made me fart all night.

Blofeld Gateau. A blend of choice and exotic fruits from all parts of the world. Much beloved by BBC commentators. Used by Bill Frindall as a paper weight and as a gag to silence Trevor Bailey.

It might surprise those who have visited my home to learn that the lady wife 'on her day' is quite a decent cook – if you like that sort of thing.

Here are are a few of her favourite dishes:
Duckworth a l'orange
Fishlock pie
Brain with braund and cranston sauce
Pridgeon pie
Roast tim lamb with tom graveny
Insole colbert
Appleyard and bobberry pie
Bannerjee curry a la modi with clive rice
Cecil parkin
Dilley con carne
Jellied ealham
Rabone steak
Winston Place and chips
Van Geloven-ready chicken
Jardines on toast
Pleass pudding
Todd in the hole
Fagg roll

Finally, I invited several well-known 'personalities' from our 'summer game' to tell their idea of the perfect meal and the perfect day to accompany it.

Here are some of their replies:

Freddie Trueman
'My idea of the perfect meal is as follows: it would be in a discreet, candlelit Bloomsbury vegetarian restaurant in the company of Margaret Drabble, Marghanita Laski, Iris Murdoch and Jill Tweedie.'

E. R.Dexter
'I can think of nothing more perfect than an evening spent in the company of my very dear friend, Michael Parkinson, in his home town of Burnley.

'After a delicious meal of beans on toast in the bus station café we would repair to the vaults bar of the Queens Hotel and there swap yarns about happy days at our respective prep schools, about carefree, languid, summer afternoons spent on punts among the dreaming spires of our alma maters and of the fun we had as young subalterns during our National Service.

'After that it would be a night dancing the hours away at the Civic Ballroom, Hoyland Common, in the company of Janet Street-Porter and Russell Harty.'

Majid Khan (brother of the well-known songwriter, Sammy)
'It's well known that I'm a sociable sort of bloke. I'd like nothing better than a night on the batter in Cardiff with the boys. I'd ring them all up – Wilf, Eifion, 'Lol', Alan, Nashy, 'Lofty' Pete Walker and all the other boozy old wankers – and I'd say: "Come on, boys, on with your drinking boots. The treat's on me."

'Then we'd get stuck into pints of Brain's Dark at The Old Arcade. Then it'd be across to Canton to give the old "Skull Attack" a bloody good thrashing.

'Then we'd get a cab and hot foot it down Tiger Bay for a good old arse-rattling curry. Then we'd all piss off back to Tony Cordle's and bugger up his Vivaldi records.'

Geoffrey Boycott

'I should throw open my official residence to a small and select group of my closest friends and admirers.

'Among those present would be: Sir Keith Joseph, Sir Geoffrey Howe, Professor Milton Keynes, Simon Rattle, Snoo Wilson, Vanessa Redgrave, Sir Arnold and Lord Goodman, Lady Antonia Frazier and her brother, Joe, Sir Cecil Beaton, Larry Olivier, Sir Douglas Bader, Sir Isiah Berlin, Mr Barry Took, Victor Gollancz, Sir George Weidenfeld and his wife, Mavis Nicholson, Queen Salote of Tonga, Senator Edward Kennedy, Lord Lucan and Miss Kitty McShane, Miss Jan Leeming, Mr Ned Sherrin, Mr Barry Cryer, Mr John Junkin, Mr Robin Bailey and his father, Trevor, Dame Petula Clark, Cliff Richard, and in contrast from the world of music, Miss Elizabeth Schwarzkopf and Miss Ann Shelton, Patrick Moore, Mr Brian Clough, Andrew Lloyd-Webber, John Julius Northwich, Lord David Cecil, Lord Carrington, the Duke of Kent, Mr Harry Pilling, Auberon Waugh and his daughter, Evelyn, Hinge and Brackett, Sir Michael Edwardes (who's small enough to come twice) and finally my mentor and dearest confidant, the one man I consider to be even greater than I at this moment in time, Mr Peter West and his mother, Dame Rebecca.

'After taking a net we would all repair to my state apartments where I would deliver the annual Sir Geoffrey Boycott Memorial Lecture, which I give every year.

'Then after taking another net and having a rub down by Bernard Thomas we would retire to the state dining rooms, where individual fish and ship suppers would be provided by Mr Harry Ramsden.

'Then after taking another net we would all have after-dinner mints like you see them doing on the television adverts.

'I wonder if I should have invited Ray Illingworth?'

Alec Bedser
'What I'd like most is an incredibly boring evening at home with my brother and a plate of sausage and chips.'

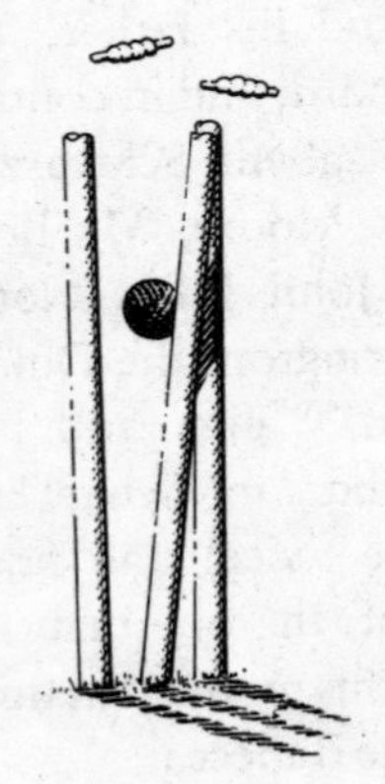

10
Polar Games

In my opinion a vast amount of unmitigated tosh, piffle and utter drivel has been written about the enmity and antipathy which existed between the two polar explorers, Scott and Amundsen.

Jealousy, hatred, deep, brooding resentment, sheer bloody-mindedness: all these emotions played their part in the intense hostility which existed between those two men.

But what caused these feelings?

Conventional canon has it that Scott's detestation of Amundsen was the direct result of the Norwegian's cheating and entering into a race for the South Pole.

Absolute balderdash.

The whole can of worms was created by one event and one event alone – a cricket match played at Cape Evans in Antarctica on 18 September 1911, between elevens representing the respective polar expeditions of Captain Scott and Roald Amundsen.

It was the ill feeling engendered by this match which caused all the subsequent virulence of passions and ultimately, in my view, the untimely death of Scott himself.

For more than fifty years this incident has been 'hushed up' by those jealous to preserve Scott's reputation as an heroic figure whose death in the snowy wastes of Antarctica was a lasting monument to the typical English qualities of manly virtue, moral courage and noble self-sacrifice.

At the same time these misguided men sought to portray Amundsen as a base and treacherous liar, a glory hunter and, above all, a cheat and a practioner of gamesmanship of the 'very worst sort'.

The facts prove otherwise.

Let them now speak for themselves.

As I sit in my study now with the lapwings wheeling and diving above the water meadows, the fat black rooks purring in the vicarage elms and the milkman's horse ambling heavily down the honeysuckled lane for all the world like Tom Goddard plodding back to his mark at Cheltenham, my mind wanders back in time, soaring weightlessly over storm-thrashed oceans, gliding gracefully over gnashing floes of ice and silent wastes of dazzling snow.

And like a great brooding skua it skims down tumbling mountain ramparts, cascading ice falls and lumbering glaciers and alights on a broken-backed wooden crate, and its glinting steely eyes survey the scene.

A hut.

Scott's hut at Cape Evans.

Scott's specially constructed hut with its score-box, its balconies for home side and visitors side, its separate entrances for gentlemen and players and the broad sweep of its long room windows.

And outside on the snow a hive of activity.

Two ponies pulling a heavy roller.

The unmistakeable figure of Petty Officer Evans erecting a sight-screen.

Captain Oates in the nets bowling his distinctive leg breaks and googlies to Lieutenant Bowers.

(How curious, incidentally, and how felicitous that Oates should share the same Christian name initials as the celebrated Kent and England wicket-keeper, Mr Leslie Ames.)

Let us not dwell on that matter, however.

Let us direct our gaze to the broad expanse of snow shining and white and pure outside Scott's hut.

Do you see?

Chief Stoker Lashly digging a popping crease and Cecil Meares feeding the remnants of a matting wicket to his beloved huskies.

All is ready for the historic match.

But wait.

Let us examine the circumstances which created this most significant event in the whole history of polar exploration.

I have in my possession documentary evidence to

prove beyond peradventure that Scott had known of Amundsen's intention to strike out for the South Pole for at least one year.

Indeed discussions and meetings had taken place between the two men at Nansen's home in Christiana.

It was at the last of these meetings that Scott came up with a proposition that was as novel as it was daring.

The two expeditions should set out for Antarctica, he suggested.

But once there they should play a cricket match.

The winners of this match would be the expedition which would strike out for the Pole.

Despite his unfamiliarity with the 'summer game', Amundsen enthusiastically accepted the challenge.

With typical Norwegian thoroughness he threw himself into the meticulous planning which was essential if the polar cricket match was to be won.

We know from the archives that in the summer of 1910 Amundsen secretly brought a party of Norwegians to Lords to be given instruction in the rudiments of cricket.

During this time Amundsen took his expert ski maker, Bjaaland, to the factories of Messrs Gunn and Moore to learn the mysteries of the time-honoured craft of cricket bat-making.

I am aware that there are academic historians with their foul-smelling socks and damp handshakes who will hotly dispute these assertions of mine.

'Fiddle de dee,' they will say. 'There was no arrangement.'

Oh, really?

Well, consider, my friends, the case of Trygve Gran.

He was Norwegian, yet he was a member of Scott's party. Why?

Historians state that Scott engaged Gran as skiing instructor to the expedition. But we know from diaries that Gran was scarcely ever employed in that capacity.

The so-called 'experts' have spent decades wondering why. Indeed a recent biographer of Scott and Amundsen has suggested that Gran's inactivity was one of the many blunders committed by Scott in his running of the ill-fated expedition.

What arrant nonsense.

Gran's role in the polar expedition in the light of our knowledge of the cricket match is blindingly obvious.

He was to be umpire.

Scott with typical English sportsmanship had decided that the umpire his team would provide would be Norwegian.

So are gestures purely altruistic in motive twisted and distorted for the sake of cheap 'sensationalism'.

Let us no longer detain ourselves with such perfidy and concentrate our attentions on the match itself.

Unfortunately, the score-book is no longer extant.

By an extreme and profoundly irritating stroke of fate it was in the hip pocket of Captain Oates when he set off on his final and heroic last journey into the polar night and eternal oblivion.

Would that he had only paused a second before opening the flap of that snowbound tent.

Would that he had considered the full implications of his dramatic gesture.

Had he done so, I am convinced that there is not the slightest doubt he would have handed over that precious score-book to his companions and would thus have been accorded by posterity even greater warmth than he now holds in our affections. Oates was indeed 'a very gallant gentleman' – but he was also damnably inconsiderate.

Another sad gap in our knowledge of this match is caused by the absence of score-cards.

We know from his diaries that Dr Edward 'Bill' Wilson illustrated in watercolour several of these cards, which were printed on the portable press specially shipped out to the Antarctic for this purpose.

Indeed the workings of this press had been a major and constant source of concern to Scott over the months of detailed planning he had made into the running of the expedition.

He had, in fact, 'borrowed' one of the score-card printing presses from Lords and in the winter of 1910 taken it to Arctic Norway for special ice trials.

It had failed dismally, but with a stubborness of spirit that was ultimately to prove his undoing Scott refused to listen to advice and insisted on bringing to the Antarctic a score-card printing press that was known to be a failure in the extremely low temperatures prevailing in that inhospitable clime.

Would that he had taken a press from Old Trafford.

Would, too, that we were able to solve the mystery of the 'missing' cards.

Theories for their loss abound.

The most likely is, I believe, the one which maintains that Scott took the score-cards with him on his final dash to the pole, intending to leave them buried in a casket at the South Pole itself to prove to the world (if proof were needed) the cultural and moral supremacy of England.

On reaching the pole and discovering that Amundsen had been there before him, Scott was devastated.

In a fit of pique he took the score-cards from the container carried on a halter round the neck of Petty Officer Evans and, ripping them to shreds with his teeth, hurled them high into the sky to be whisked away by the polar gales and buried forever in the snowy deserts, which were later to entomb him and his companions with fatal results.

No, we have no 'facts and figures' about the match, and so we must rely on the diaries and letters of those who were present.

We know, for example, from his diaries that Scott had been brooding with deep misgivings about the match for many months after the departure of the *Terra Nova* from England.

He wrote:

'Everything that could be done to ensure the success of our party has been done. We are a fine body of men, resolute in purpose, steadfast in spirit. Our equipment is the finest that could be devised. We have ponies, tractors and dogs. We have men trained in every facet of the scientific skills. We have old polar hands who have experienced every one of the unimaginable hardships and terrors that mother nature will hurl at us. Yet one nagging doubt remains – where is our off-spinner and where is our second change seamer?'

Others, too, had their fears.

Oates writing to his mother in his typical graphic and unpunctuated style said:

'We are a pretty dismal lot we are all willing but where is the leadership? We have absolutely no experience of cricket in polar regions, yet Scott refuses point blank to organize decent nets, and what infuriates me even more is that we have on board *Terra Nova* a biologist name of Lillie. He's a fast bowler of rare old promise yet Scott with typical idocy refuses to allow him to join the shore party. Madness.'

Madness? Stubborness?

Or was Scott by deliberately refusing the services of a man who was to become one of the greatest fast bowlers the 'summer game' has ever know, showing manifestations of the propensity for self-destruction which would later end with such tragic results?

Even Bowers – loyal, uncomplaining, hard-working gallant little 'Birdie' Bowers – had his misgivings.

When he saw Amundsen and his team arrive at Cape Evans for the match, he wrote to his mother:

'Scott is a topper – a better leader or tent companion one could not have. I can say unhesitatingly tht he is one of the best – an absolute sahib. But when I look at the gear and the togs the Norwegians have brought for the match, I admit the old heart plummets right to the boots.'

Those words were prophetic indeed.

The Norwegians' equipment was certainly impres-

Specially prepared wax for their skis and cricket bats, quick-release bindings for their cricket pads, extra-long, non-corrosive crampons for their cricket boots, and warm comforting reindeer-fur lining for their abdominal protectors – the Norwegians had 'done their homework'.

If that were not enough to cast a cloud over the minds of the English team, worse was to follow when a bitter dispute broke out betweeen Scott and Amundsen over the use of dogs and horses.

Scott had shipped out ponies especially for the pulling of the heavy roller.

Amundsen refused to allow that. He had brought his huskies, and he insisted that they be allowed to pull the heavy roller.

The argument raged.

Finally, it was agreed that trials should take place to test the relative merits of dog and pony.

Let Scott's diaries speak for themselves.

As he sat on the players' balcony of the hut at Cape Evans watching the ponies pulling the heavy roller he wrote:

'It is pathetic to see the ponies floundering in the soft patches. Now and again they have to stop, and it is horrid to see them half engulfed in the snow, panting and heaving from the strain.'

Amundsen's huskies, however, when put to the test, simply skimmed over the surface of the snow, the heavy roller whirring gaily in their wake.

Once more the months of meticulous preparation

had paid their dividends, for Amundsen had the previous winter spent four months with his dogs on the high, bleak snow plateaux of Telemark, training them to pull heavy roller and gang mower.

Scott never forgave Amundsen for this public humiliation, especially as at the end of the day together with Oates, Wilson, Bowers and Edgar Evans he was compelled to 'manhaul' the heavy roller.

Under those inauspicious circumstances it was not unexpected that Scott lost the toss.

'Bill' Wilson, his sturdy and steadfast confidant, tried hard to cheer him up, but he was inconsolable.

'I fear the worst, Bill,' he said. 'I fear we are done for.'

How apt his misgivings seemed as on the most perfect of wickets the Norwegians totted up a score of major proportions.

From the diary of 'Birdie' Bowers we know that he himself caught out Wisting from the bowling of Atkinson for seventy-eight.

We know, too, how to Scott's fury Gran turned down his lbw appeal against, chagrin of chagrin, his opposite skipper, Amundsen, who subsequently went on to score 175 – although some historians maintain that his score was, in fact, 174 owing to Gran's failure to signal a 'short run'.

We do not know the exact Norwegian score, although I suspect it was nearer to 600 than 700.

What we do know, however, is that as soon as Scott's Eleven went into bat they were stricken by the most appalling weather. Blizzards, gales, lashing hail storms and sub-zero temperatures turned the wicket into a real 'sticky dog', and in next to no time Scott's side, finding

Helmer Hanssen virtually unplayable, were in dire straits at 78 for 8 with Oates ret. hurt, bad feet.

It was at this moment that the ultimate tragedy occurred.

The weather closed in so badly that play was no longer possible. Day after day after day the vile polar weather did its worst.

Scott wrote in his diary:

'Dear God, this place is terrible. Worse by far than the Thursday of an Old Trafford Test.'

But worse was indeed to follow.

In the negotiations that had taken place before the match Scott had insisted that his expedition would be responsible for supplies.

Reluctantly Amundsen had agreed, but only on the condition that if supplies failed, Scott would forfeit the match.

Supplies began to run out.

The special depot built on the long leg boundary could not be reached owing to the severity of the weather, and stores in the hut began to run dangerously low.

On the fourth day the cucumber sandwiches ran out.

By the fifth day there was no egg and cress, and on the seventh day the last of the maids of honour was consumed.

With the tea urn dip stick no longer registering, Amundsen took action.

He demanded that either Scott replenish the stores by making an immediate dash to the long leg depot, or he would insist that the match be forfeited.

With the ponies useless for such a task Scott and his

four companions set out to man haul the sledge to the depot and its supplies of swiss rolls, pilchard paste and gentleman's relish.

The journey there and back took ten days – ten days of the most appalling hardships and deprivations which Scott and his gallant band bore with a courage that was almost superhuman.

But when they got back, Amundsen had gone – and he had claimed victory.

The next Scott was to hear of him was when he reached the South Pole and there found the flag of Norway flying from Amundsen's Gunn and Moore cricket bat.

It was the ultimate humiliation.

So there is 'the true story'.

For more than five decades it has been hushed up for one reason and one reason alone – the fact that Norway defeated England at cricket.

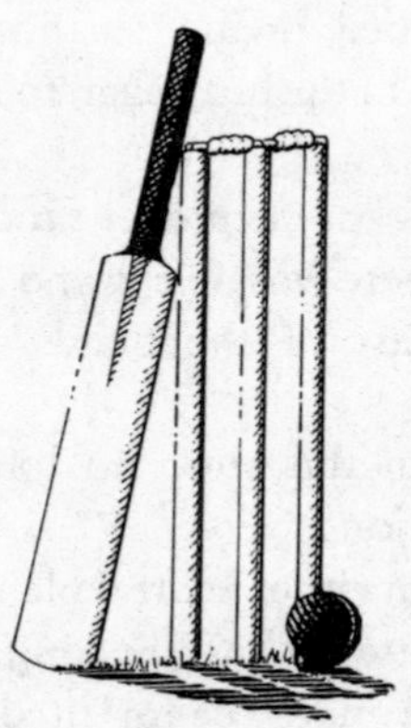

11
The Ones That Got Away

Just recently there has come into my possession a trunkful of priceless cricket memorabilia.

Among the many items of immeasurable and overpowering interest in this positive Pandora's chest of cricketing nostalgia are:

Mr D. R. Jardine's personal toenail clippers; a portion of Mr Peter West's left sock discovered in fossil remains in the BBC commentary box at Trent Bridge; a half-sucked Malteser, property of J. J. Warr Esq. (the other half, I believe is in the possession of The Trustees The Robin Marlar Appreciation Society, Car Park Attendants' Branch); and a first edition of the very rare E. W. Swanton book, *On The Hippy Trail to Katmandu.*

But of all the treasures the one which pleases me most is the dust-laden file, stained with Cooper's marmalade and Brown and Robertson's damson jam, which contains a series of obituaries, which, for one reason or another, never appeared in Wisden.

I propose to present to you an alphabetical selection of these sublimely precious examples of literature of the 'summer game'.

A 'Fong, Horace. Born Shanghai, June 1907. Considered by many to have been the finest Chinese left-handed opening bat of his generation. Leading member of the 'gang of four' who transformed Chinese cricket in the post Go AI Len era. Leader of the left-handed revolution in 1960s with I Kin, What Ton and Pull Ar. Executed Ba Cup 1969.

Bunch, Herbert Neville. Born Alston Junction, August 1878. Found dead on a train outside Tamworth (Low Level) station. He was wearing a fireman's helmet, sequined G-string and pink patent-leather dancing pumps.

Coats-Stufffley, Winston Foden. Born Gibson-beyond-Cardus, 17 October 1901. Hon. Sec. Faroes Cricket Society, 1932-37. Died at sea, 1929.

Dabson, Robert Falcon. Born Warrington, September 1888. Distinguished scorer and mountaineer. First man to make a single-handed ascent of the south face of the Warner Stand.

Evans, Gareth Dylan Gwynfor Mostyn Bismarck. Welsh cricket professional. Born Felinfoel, 1915. Died of drink Vale of Neath, 1931.

Fudge, Granville. Born May 1900. Forceful right-hand bat and fast medium left arm bowler. Played five seasons for Worcestershire. The only player ever to score three successive first-class centuries while wearing ladies underwear. Great friend of Bunch Herbert Neville (CV). Died Tangiers, 1975.

Golightly, Harriet. Born Christopher St Martins, July 1918. Sister of Ben Golightly, official scorecard printer to Queen Wilhemina Henrietta of the Netherlands. Ladies champion, Throwing the Cricket Ball, 1936-39. Accomplished contortionist. Died in a cricket bag, Fenners, 1943.

Hancock, Thomas. Born Marlborough, May 1786. Died London, March 1865. Inventor and manufacturer who founded the British rubber industry and thus gained the undying gratitude of countless generations of Australian cricket tourists to England. His chief invention, 'the masticator', worked rubber scraps into a shredded mass of rubber that could be worked into blocks or rolled into sheets. This process, perfected in 1821, led to a partnership with the Scottish chemist and inventor of waterproof fabrics, Charles Macintosh. The best known of the waterproof articles they produced were macintosh coats, popularly known as Mackintoshes. In his memory a statue was erected at the back of the Harry Makepeace Memorial Bicycle Sheds, Old Trafford.

Inkpen, Mervyn Alsager. Born Melbourne, March 1927. Doctor distinguished for his research into injuries resulting from the cricket field. Discoverer of 'off-spinners' hip' and 'Leg slips' hemmorroids'. Killed by falling sightscreen, Brisbane, 1957.

Jutter, Ernest Offenbach. Born Batavia 1918. Treasurer Musicians' Cricket Society, 1947-77. Composer of Ballet Suite, 'A Night with Nureyev, a Day with James Langridge.'

Kilknockin, Harry Montague Devenish, Third Earl of. Born Newport, IOW, November 1899. Wicket-keeper for Eton, Balliol, Gentlemen of Ireland and House of Lords Strollers. Maj. Gen. F. K. St J. L-B-W writes:
' "Stinky" Kilknockin achieved cricketing immortality with his unfailing, unbounding sense of humour, his ability to "stick to the task" whatever the cost and the constant and nauseous stench to his socks. I have no hesitation in stating that Kilknockin's socks were the most revolting objects I have encountered in a lifetime's devotion to the "summer game" and all matters pertaining. The cleanliness of teeth, too, left a "lot to be desired" and his nose was remarkable for the number of hairs protruding therefrom. His eating habits, too, were notorious for their loathesomeness and his sexual proclivities were detested by all those who had the misfortune to suffer from his attentions. He was also a "more than adequate" middle order batsman.'

Lugg, Bert. Born Arlott-by-Keating, February 1856. West country cricketing wit and raconteur. Author of *A Golden Treasury of Cricketing Parlance* and *John and Mary Whitehouse, A Warwickshire Romance.* Died 1949, Melford St Swantons.

Maharabhindi, Maharajah of. Friend and confidant of the great Earl Mountbatman, the man who captained England in 867 Test matches, scored the greatest number of first-class centuries, achieved 'the double' on no less than seventy-nine occasions, won the Ashes single-handedly with one great bound five times and was the father of Sir Jack Hobbs, Sir Donald Bradman and Mr B. D. 'Bomber'Wells. Also winner of 'Mastermind' on six successive occasions.

Newt, Hector Ian. Scottish cricketer. Born Peebles, 1906. Died Titmus, 1976.

O'Casey, Sean. Born Dublin, 30 March 1880. Irish playwright and enthusiast of the 'summer game'. Author of the two definitive cricket dramas, 'Juno and the Pocock', and 'Shadow of a Bradman'.

Ponting, Herbert G. Official photographer on all Sir Dereck Shackleton's expeditions to the polar regions. Famous for his pictures of the harrowing hardships suffered by all on the Dexter Expedition to West Indies, 1963. Illustrator of the Sainsbury and Horton edition of *The Ingoldsby-Mackenzie Legends*.

Quirck, Graham. Born Perth, 1928. Collapsed in the gents toilet during an interval in the match Western Australia versus Queensland, 1959, and when carried into the pavilion life was found to be extinct. Antipodean cricket correspondent for many years to *Exchange and Mart*. Joint Nobel Prize Winner for Scoring with Bill Frindall, 1958. Perspired excessively.

Rust, Sydney George. A well-loved and much-imitated

'character' for five decades at Bramall Lane. Lord Hawke writes: 'Rust was a capital fellow.'

Sellows-Hoffmann, Hugo Ralph. Born Trinidad, 1911. Architect of cricket pavilions. Designer of the unsinkable patrons bar, Hove (1937). Talented painter noted for his sight-screen *trompe l'oeils*. Of particular merit are his 'Madonna and Child opening the innings, Buxton' and his immortal 'The Purification of Binks, Headingley'.

Tattenhall, Clayton Geoffrey. Famous groundsman. Born Sowerbutts-in-Tyldesleydale, 1901. Breeder of the quick crop radish to be grown on Old Trafford pitches during rain-stopped-play intervals. Moved to Gloucester where he invented the moveable batting order now known as 'The Rotation of Crapps'.

U, Nu. See Nu, U.

Voigt, Conrad Arthur. Died on 9 January 1939, appeared 'a few times' in the Buckinghamshire Second Eleven. A good defensive batsman, he was particularly strong on the off side. W. W. H. writes: 'Voigt was a good defensive batsman, particularly strong on the off side.'

Xenophen. Greek philosopher. Died Attercliffe, 350 BC. Originator of the philosophy that only men of native birth may play for Yorkshire.

Yapp, Llewellyn. Welsh patriot. Born Pontyboyce, February 1902. Translator into Welsh of *Wisden's Almanack* and E.W. Swanton's *On The Hippy Trail to Pontymister*. Died of boredom during Mr Tony

Lewis's benefit year.

Zog, Albania, ex-King of. An absolute stinker. *See also* Tinniswood, Peter.

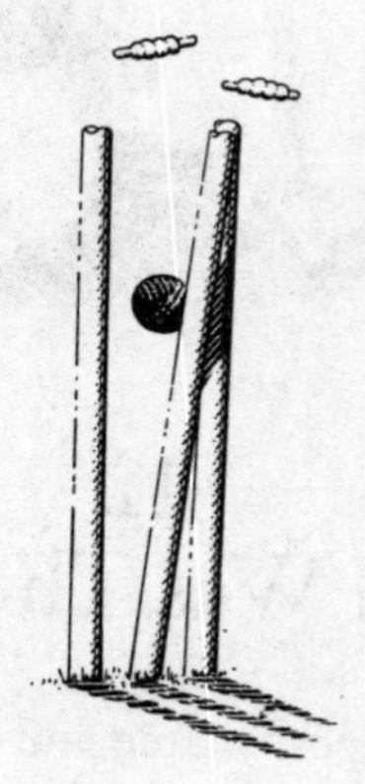

12
I Was There

It is with the deepest shame and sense of misery that I have to admit it – yes, I was there.

On the greatest day of infamy in our 'summer game' it was my profound misfortune to be present and, indeed, play a central part in the wretched proceedings which so marred and scarred the Saturday of the Centenary Test at Lords.

Let us be quite clear about one thing:

In no way do I condone the attitude of those spectators who abused and in some cases physically assaulted the two umpires on the steps of the pavilion.

While I have considerable sympathy with the views of those who maintain that anyone who has the effrontery to look like Mr Harold 'Dicky' Bird (or even to be Mr Harold 'Dicky' Bird) deserves to be given a thorough thrashing every morning of his life, I believe that these feelings should never be allowed public expression – especially at 'headquarters'.

While I believe, too, that the England captain, Mr Ian Botham, has the looks and the manner of a recently made redundant chef on a British Rail dining car, and that his Australian counterpart, Mr Ian Chappell, bears a remarkable resemblance to a cheroot-toting lieutenant colonel in some vile-smelling Central American republic, this gives no licence to express outright contempt towards them.

However, when all is said and done, and, although it pains me to the core of my soul to say it, on the day in question it is easy to understand and to forgive the baseness of behaviour of everyone concerned.

And it is even easier to point the finger at those responsible for such ghastliness.

The guilty ones must be named.

They are none other than 'the authorities'.

They and they alone must take full responsibility for the 'day of infamy'.

And why?

Because basic common sense should have told them that their actions could have done nothing else than provoke unseemly violence, outright mutiny and rowdyism of a type only normally seen at an annual conference of the Conservative and Unionist party.

Putting it quite simply – it was just asking for trouble locking me in the pavilion gents urinals with Mr K. D. 'Slasher' Mackay.

From that and from nothing else stemmed what will forever be known in the annals of our 'summer game' as 'The Troubles'.

As calmly as I can I shall now describe the events of that fateful day.

As always on the Saturday of the Lords Test I arose at three thirty in the morning so as not to disturb the lady wife and her confounded Bedlington terriers and made my way in stockinged feet through the rose shrubberies where friends were waiting for me with 'a fast car'.

How comforting the clink of brandy flask.

How heady the scent of fine malt whisky.

How beautiful the unfolding panorama of our dear English countryside as dawn spread her rosy fingers over pasture and water meadow, over mist-shrouded cattle and sentinel heron, over slumbering thatch and sputtering rill.

We arrived at our club in good time for breakfast.

How comforting the clink of brandy flask.

How heady the scent of malt whisky.

How the gastric juices quickened to the tang of sizzling gammon, plump sausages, butter-drenched mushroom, spitting kidney, snarling steak, tight-coiled chop and purring, golden eggs.

How the palate crooned to the caress of rich and noble claret.

And how comforting the clink of brandy flask and how heady the scent of fine malt whisky.

And then to Lords.

Lords in all its finery.

Lords *en fête*.

Lords ablaze in the glory of distinguished Test

cricketers, both old and young.

What a panopoly of talent.

I spotted at once Lord Harris and Sir Jack Hobbs, and within the hour had seen and spoken to such luminaries as Alec Bedser, Eric Bedser, Alec Bedser, Eric Bedser, and a gloomy fellow in shapeless grey suit and nylon socks who looked remarkably like Alec Bedser and his brother, Eric.

The first hint of trouble came when I found a man of unmistakeable colonial appearance ensconced in my chair in the Brian Close Memorial Bar in the pavilion.

He was dressed in a wide-brimmed hat with one side affixed to the crown, snuff-stained khaki drill jacket, navy blue PT shorts and hiker's boots and seemed to be under the impression that I was called 'Blue'.

Dodging the brown stream of chewing tobacco which squirted from the side of his mouth, I examined the badge on the lapel of his drill jacket and discovered that the brute was none other than Mr Keith Miller's grandmother.

I summoned Griffiths from his office to remove the creature, and in the ensuing fracas received a severe bite on my left buttock and had the clasp of an MCC cufflink buckled beyond redemption.

This was to prove a minor irritation in the light of subsequent events.

After settling myself in my chair (somewhat painfully I am bound to confess) I summoned the head waiter, Bailey, to fetch me a bottle of my usual Brown and Robertson vintage tawny port.

'Sorry, sir,' said the lugubrious, obsequious Bailey, 'We've sold out.'

'Sold out?' I bellowed.

'Yes, sir,' said Bailey. 'Not a bottle left in the place.'

In the ensuing fracas I received superficial flesh wounds on both elbows, and had the point of an MCC tie-pin most painfully embedded two inches to the sou' sou' east of my left nipple.

What could have turned into a most 'ugly scene' was curtailed by an announcement that there would be no play before luncheon.

The cheer which went up in the bar was indicative of the relief felt by one and all that our imbibing activities would not be disturbed by the necessity of having to watch a cricket match which to one and all was an irritating diversion to the main purpose of the event – the reunion of old friends and colleagues, the swapping of yarns and badinage and the celebration of one hundred years of incredibly boring cricket articles written by Mr E. W. 'Gloria' Swanton.

As we looked anxiously at the lowering clouds one question was uppermost in our minds – would the bloody things suddenly lift, dry out the pitch and so completely spoil our day?

It was in the manner shown by generation of Englishmen beleaguered in rotting Flanders trench, steamy African jungle and Tesco cash desk that with stiff upper lips and steely eyes we faced this danger.

I found myself in the company of a dwarf-like figure with large ears name of Hazlitt or Harsnett or Hassett who claimed to have captained his country at Test match level.

To me he looked more like an undertaker suffering from a chronic attack of piles, and I felt bound to appraise him of my views.

In the ensuing fracas I received a stinging blow behind the right temple and was damn near garrotted by Mr Geoffrey Boycott's jock strap.

However, once again fate intervened in the form of another announcement on the public address system to the effect that the museum at the back of the pavilion was shortly to be opened with an exhibition of Mr Gil Langley's underpants.

Chairs were overturned, tables were knocked asunder as eager members fought and scratched with each other to gain a favourable place at the head of the queue outside the museum.

Peace, blessed peace, reigned in the bar.

Once more united with my friends, I established myself at a strategic point near the entrance to the gents urinals and soon we were soothing our tattered nerves with generous supplies of an excellent 1974 Schloss Blofeld Spätauslese.

It was during this blissful lull that I and my friends heard the words which sent shivers of fear and mortification rilling down the length of our respective spines.

In a dark corner of the bar, standing next to the space invader machines, were two figures clad in white coats, one of whom was drinking Vimto out of a large panama hat.

The umpires!

And they were deep in conversation.

We held our breath.

We strained our ears.

And then we heard those terrifying words:

'Right then, Dicky. We'll tell them – we resume play

immediately after lunch.'

In the ensuing fracas I received several sharp kicks in my private parts and was set upon by several burly men who smelled strongly of fresh score cards and Tavener's fruit drops.

Despite my frenzied protestations and struggles I was forcibly thrown into the gents urinals and there as I slid and slithered on the tiled floor I heard the unmistakable sound of a padlock being applied to the outside of the door.

I leapt to my feet.

I hammered at the door.

I heaved at the handle.

I shouted. I bellowed.

All to no avail.

I was locked in.

And then suddenly I was aware of another's presence.

I turned.

And there placidly standing at a stall attending to a 'call of nature' was none other than Mr K. D. 'Slasher' Mackay of Queensland and Australia.

To see him standing there so cool, calm and collected set off a chain of emotions in me, which to this day remain blurred and confused.

Suffice it to say that in the ensuing fracas several articles of a plumbing nature were detached from the walls of the urinal and I was knocked into oblivion by a particularly large Edrich and Compton patent ballcock.

How long I remained unconscious I do not know.

I remember waking slowly to hear on the public address system an announcement that owing to unfortunate and unforeseen circumstances in the pavilion the entire urinal facilities of the ground had been rendered inoperative.

The effect was instantaneous.

Imagine it – twenty to thirty thousand healthy red-blooded English males denied an outlet for one of the most basic and fundamental of human needs.

Thus the outcry.

Thus the uproar.

Thus the assault on umpires.

Thus the abuse of committee members of MCC.

Thus the clamour and the violence.

Thus the fact that despite the appearance of strong sunshine and a brisk drying wind in mid-afternoon, the pitch remained sodden.

Well, there was only one place available for the twenty to thirty thousand healthy, red-blooded English males to. . .

I was there.

Oh yes, I was there.

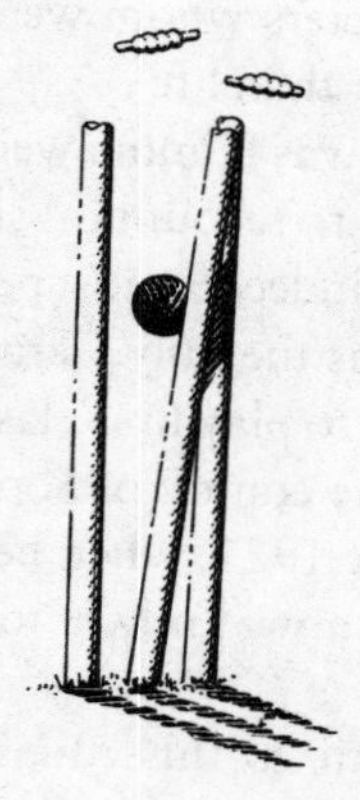

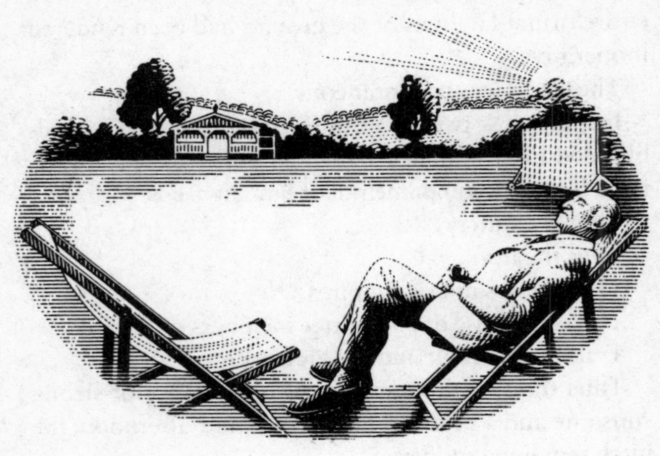

13
Incident at Frome

Our beloved 'summer game' abounds in stories and anecdotes of characters whom we cricket lovers traditionally term 'larger than life'.

Such a character was Himmelweit.

It is my intention to recount his singular history.

And 'singular' is indeed a most pertinent word to use, for Himmelweit was the only German in the history of the 'summer game' to play first-class county cricket.

He played for the county of Somerset from the year 1919 until the year 1921, when he became the central figure in what is now known to historians as 'The incident at Frome'.

Himmelweit came to this country in the year 1916

when his Zeppelin was shot down during a bombing raid on Shepton Mallet – thus giving him residential qualifications to play for Somerset.

He was deposited forthwith into prison – thus giving him residential qualifications to play for Wormwood Scrubs.

He first came to the notice of the cricketing authorities when he appeared in the match, Minor Counties versus Huns, at Much Wenlock.

Minor Counties were skippered by Jas Humberstone senior.

Huns were skippered by Thomas Mann, a minor literary figure, who was later to achieve wider fame as the father and grandfather respectively of F. G. and F. T. Mann of Middlesex and England.

Minor Counties won the toss and elected to bat.

The innings was opened by Jas Humberstone, Senior, and the former Leicestershire professional, Amiss, later to achieve wider fame as the father and grandfather respectively of the two cricketing brothers, Dennis and Kingsley.

The Huns skipper tossed the crimson rambler to Himmelweit to open the bowling.

Humberstone crouched at the crease in his typical aggressive stance, and as he faced to the bowling the buckles of his braces flashed angrily, the ferrets in his hip pocket gnashed their teeth and the clank of steel dentures echoed round the ground.

'Right, Fritz,' he growled. 'Do your worst.'

It was to be one of the most memorable moments in the history of the 'summer game'.

Himmelweit commenced his run.

One stride, two strides, three strides.

It was indeed a fearsome sight as his iron crosses clattered and his cavalry sabre splintered the weak Shropshire sunlight into myriads of sparkling fragments.

Nearer and nearer he approached the wicket, and as he did so spectators became aware of a curious whistling sound.

Louder and louder it grew.

Ghastly.

Horrendous.

A banshee howl that caused spectators to clasp their ears in agony, for all the world like the unsuspecting audience at a Cliff Richard concert.

And then Himmelweit reached the wicket and delivered the ball. It was a masterly delivery; full length, pitched on middle and leg and veering sharply to off with a snakelike whiplash.

Humberstone's castle was wrecked.

That well-known cricket writer, Mr Neville Cardew, later to achieve even wider fame as the father and grandfather respectively of the distinguished wit and raconteur, Mr Cardew Robinson, wrote in his journal the following:

'I doubt whether any man alive – or dead – could have played that ball.

'Even though Humberstone at the moment of delivery was stretched on the ground writhing in contortions of agony, hands clamped tight to his auditory orifices, I am of the firm opinion that the perfect pitch and pace of the ball would have beaten his forward defensive prod and caused him forthwith to give no trouble to the scorer.'

Thus did the carnage begin.

The Minor Counties were dismissed for five, Himmelweit taking all ten wickets at a cost of only one run, this being solely due to a piece of grossly negligent ground fielding by the young Otto Klemperer.

The Huns in the person of their two openers, the Umlaut brothers, A. P. F. and J. W. H. N. S. – the latter known affectionately as Johnny Will Heute Nicht Schlagen – knocked off the runs required in one over thus winning the match by ten wickets.

The Minor Counties players were incensed, but it was some time later during the subsequent fracas in the tea tent that the source of the whistling sound, which had caused them so much distress, was discovered.

Himmelweit, with typical Teutonic baseness of behaviour, had affixed to the inside of his kneecap a device used by the German gunners in their howitzers during the bombardment of Beauvais to strike terror into the hearts of the Allied horses.

This prompted Humberstone, senior's, celebrated remark:

'It might not have done much for the horses, but, by God, it frightened the living shits out of me.'

Dear Jas Humberstone. But for the vileness of his tongue and his total lack of Christian charity he would have made a spendid archbishop of Canterbury – he had exactly the right size of shifty, untrustworthy eyes.

To return to Much Wenlock; the shock waves of this incident reverberated throughout the land.

Questions were asked in Parliament. A meeting of the Privy Council was summoned. All the regiments of the Scottish Highland Division were put on immediate alert, and Mrs Mary Whitehouse wrote a letter of protest to Mr Billy Cotton, junior, father and grandfather of the celebrated golfer, Joseph, and the distinguished moving kinematograph star, Henry.

As a result of all this activity there was formulated what is now known to historians of the 'summer game' as the Much Wenlock Amendment.

I quote:

'The implements of the game.

'Note Seven B.

'Articles of ordnance or artillery may not normally be used during the course of the match except by the prior agreement of the two captains, who must notify forthwith the umpires, if the said articles contain matter of an explosive nature which may cause distress or injury to domestic animals and agricultural livestock in the immediate vicinity of the ground.'

Despite the various unpleasantnesses which resulted from this match, Himmelweit's services were eagerly sought by all the first-class counties with the exception of Yorkshire, of course, who still to this day refuse to allow players of German birth or independent nature to play for the county.

It was left to MCC to decide that the enforced landing of Himmelweit's Zeppelin on Somerset soil gave that county the right to claim his services.

This rule is still in operation with a suitable amendment to deal with the accidental landing of flying saucers and the alien beings contained therein.

(It is believed that Northamptonshire have benefited most in recent times from this amendment.)

Himmelweit's deeds with Somerset require little embellishment from me.

The records speak for themselves.

Let us dwell for a moment on matters of a more personal nature.

I myself met Himmelweit personally on numerous occasions, and I can say without fear or flattery that of all the county cricketers of his era he was without doubt the most offensive and nauseating man it has ever been my misfortune to encounter.

The stiff bow of the head when he was introduced, the clicking of heels and the guttural growlings from the back of the throat seemed totally inappropriate from a first-class county cricketer – although some years later, I am bound to confess, it was made acceptable by the behaviour of Mr E. R. Dexter on entering the television commentary box at 'headquarters'.

There were times, also, when it seemed Himmelweit went out of his way to antagonize both team mate and opponent alike.

While the majority of players were content during drinks intervals to accept orange or grapefruit crush, Himmelweit insisted on a half bottle of lightly chilled Bernkasteler Niersteiner Domtal.

And on finishing this he would invariably hurl his glass to the ground and grind it underfoot with his spurs – an act which was subsequently found to be the cause of the untimely demise of the groundsman's horse at Cheltenham.

While most players, too, were content to take a light salad during the luncheon adjournment, Himmelweit insisted on a full five-course meal consisting of Bauernschmeiss mit Knackwurst, Sauerkraut mit Bratkartoffeln, Bayerische Obsttorte, Kaffee mit Schlag and Kirschknoedel à la mode Harry Makepeace.

Himmelweit fell foul of umpires, too, by insisting on appealing in his native tongue.

'Wie ist das?' he would shout in a blood-curdling yell.

And when he came to the wicket to take guard, he would scowl at the umpire and growl:

'Mittel und Bein.'

Many years later when talking about this the celebrated umpire, Mr George Pope, who was later to achieve wider fame as the father and grandfather respectively of the two Popes, John Paul 1 and John Paul 11, was heard to remark:

'Ah'd 'ave let t'booger rot, if he'd not 'ad decency to say *bitte sch*ön.'

I am indebted for this anecdote to the delightful memoirs of that most subtle of cricket writers, Mr Alan Gibson, father of Althea Gibson, the first black player ever to win a Wimbledon championship.

Himmelweit was never popular in his adopted county.

Somerset is an essentially rural county and many people in the Taunton area were convinced that it was Himmelweit with his Teutonic ways who was responsible in the winter of 1920 for a particularly severe outbreak of swine fever.

Certainly it was these suspicions which accounted for his singular lack of support from county members at the time of the infamous 'Incident at Frome'.

I now propose to recount in some detail the circumstances surrounding this occurrence.

It took place during the match against Lancashire who at that time if memory serves me correct (and it usually doesn't) were in strong contention for the county championship.

The Red Rose county had a team of all the talents, including that nonpareil of fast bowlers, the Australian, Mr E. A. McDonald, who was later to achieve even wider fame in the moving kinematograph as the partner of Mr Nelson Eddy.

McDonald was a bowler of awesome speed, a man in the prime of his talents and feared and respected the length and breadth of the country.

The match promised to be a 'humdinger'.

Somerset won the toss, and skipper, Bertie Furze, deliberated long and hard before deciding to bat on a green and lively wicket, expecting, no doubt, Himmelweit to take his toll later in the game.

It was a disastrous decision.

McDonald, bowling at fearsome speed, had the ball rearing and spitting from the very first moment of the game.

Within the space of five overs he had claimed six Somerset wickets and dispatched three of his opponents to hospital suffering from shock, head wounds and indecent exposure.

It was at this moment that Himmelweit appeared at the wicket wearing garb of the most singular appearance.

The Lancashire skipper objected immediately.

The rule book was consulted, but on finding that there was no reference to the wearing of cavalry breast plates, spiked helmets and spurs, play was allowed to continue.

The first ball McDonald bowled to Himmelweit whistled down to a good length and reared like a mortar shell head high.

Himmelweit did not flinch. Instead of ducking he soared into the air and with a movement of the head muscles that would not have disgraced the immortal 'Dixie' Dean, later to achieve even wider fame as the sister of the celebrated light comedienne and chanteuse, Miss Phyllis Dixie, headed the ball first bounce to the boundary.

Incensed, McDonald hurled down a ball of even greater speed.

Once more Himmelweit rose in the air and headed the ball to the boundary.

A six!

McDonald ground his teeth and next ball bowled a vicious delivery that hurtled at Himmelweit's midriff and struck him a sickening blow in the vitals.

Himmelweit stood his ground.

His upper lip curled icily.

The sunlight flashed on his monocle.

And then in a sudden movement he made a crucial adjustment to his dress by covering his vitals with his cavalryman's spiked helmet.

McDonald scowled and bowled again.

Another ferocious ball hurled straight at the most tender of anatomical parts known to man – and sometimes to women.

Clang!

The noise echoed and reverberated the length and breadth of the green and rolling hills of Somerset.

Rooks flew up in alarm, rabbits scurried to their burrows, hens stopped laying, but Himmelweit did not budge.

Defiant and upright he stood.

But where was the ball?

It was the great Dick Tyldesley who spotted it.

It was impaled on the end of the spike on the cavalryman's helmet.

'How's that?' he yelled.

Scarcely had the words left his lips than Himmelweit commenced his run.

'Lauf!' he shouted to his bemused partner, the young Goblet. 'Lauf, englischer Schweinhund!'

For some time the Lancashire players stood in a motionless daze as Himmelweit and his partner commenced to run between the wickets, the ball still attached to the spike on the German's helmet.

Twenty-seven they ran before the immortal Cec Parkin shouted:

'Right, lads. Let's scrag the German sod.'

The subsequent fracas was ghastly to behold.

Lancashire players piled themselves on top of Himmelweit who in cold fury struck out with his sabre.

The gore flowed copiously, and it was not until the arrival of a detachment of the Somerset Light Yeomanry and representatives of the Frome Temperance Fire Brigade that the players were separated.

There was a moment's silence.

And then the immortal Cec Parkin pounced once more.

Pointing at the wicket he shouted:

'How's that?'

Miraculously despite all the violence and the ill feeling the wicket had remained intact – except for the off bail which lay at the side of the popping crease with, entwined around it, an iron cross.

'Out,' said the umpire.

And that to my knowledge is first and only time the dismissal has been written in the scorebook:

'Out. Iron Cross hit wicket.'

But what of Himmelweit?

Of him there was no sign.

Indeed he was never seen again.

Rumour has it that he was taken under armed escort by the Somerset Light Yeomanry to London in the dead of night and there executed by firing squad on the real tennis courts at Lords.

But who can say?

One thing, however, still puzzles me about Himmelweit.

No one ever knew his Christian name.

But then, I don't suppose he was the sort of man to have one.

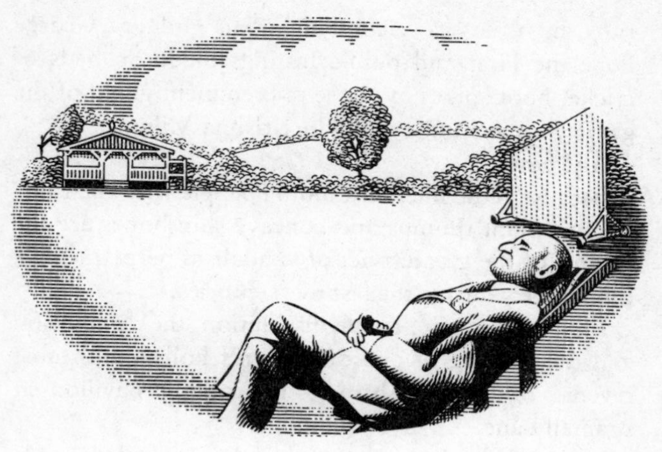

14
Witney Scrotum

It is a fact well known to all lovers of our dear 'summer game' that the inhabitants of cities and large conurbations north of a line drawn from the Bristol Channel to the Wash are without exception shiftless louts with weak chins and smokers' coughs, mean-lipped wives and slack-jawed children, all of whom, regardless of their place of birth, speak with Birmingham accents and eat with their mouths open.

I am not a prejudiced man.

I am prepared most readily to except from these strictures the city of Sheffield, whose inhabitants deserve the special sympathy of the whole nation.

On their behalf candles should be lit, church bells

rung, high masses celebrated by His Holiness George Pope the First and public fastings made on beds of cricket boot spikes by those two eminent gurus of the game, Swami Rumsey and the Krishna Milburn.

And why?

Because these fine, upstanding people with their distinctive blunt thumbs and concave shin bones are the victims of the greatest act of vandalism perpetrated in this country during the last five centuries.

I refer, of course, to the dissolution, the desecration and the sacking of one of Britain's holiest and most revered of ancient shrines – the cricket pavilion at Bramall Lane.

I am not a prejudiced man, but the scum responsible for the execution of this monstrous wickedness deserve the ultimate punishment known to civilized society – a day's incarceration in the Trent Bridge radio commentary box with Mr Tony Lewis and Mr Trevor Bailey.

Why do I state these opinions so unequivocally?

Old age, dear readers, old age.

As a body grows older and the juices run thinner and bleak winter gardens show fewer and fewer signs of approaching spring and desire withers in the nether regions of the popping crease, so do subtle changes take place within the mind.

In my case, for example (as in the case of many others of my acquaintance), I find that I now consider that everyone under the age of forty, man, woman, child and beast alike, looks exactly like Mr H. D. 'Dicky' Bird.

Indeed in moments of the darkest despair I feel that everyone over the age of forty, man, woman, child and beast alike, looks exactly like Mr H. D. 'Dicky' Bird.

Can you imagine the ghastliness induced by this state of mind?

Think of its implications.

The Miss World Championship is won by Mr H. D. 'Dicky' Bird.

Our own dear and precious Miss Una Stubbs looks like Mr H. D. 'Dicky' Bird.

So do Miss Lionel Blair, the Chief Rabbi, the Queen of the Belgians and the lady from the village dog biscuit shop.

Dear God, even Ching Ching, the panda, looks like Mr H. D. 'Dicky' Bird – small wonder, therefore, that successful mating did not take place with Mr N. Nanan of Trinidad and Nottinghamshire.

Under these circumstances I console myself more and more with my bottles of Brown and Robertson vintage tawny port, my half-scale Meccano models of Mr K. D. 'Slasher' MacKay and the knowledge that one at least of Britain's most noble institutions is still prospering.

I refer, of course, to the English village.

Here, thriving in all their rampant glory, are some of the finest flowerings of the English way of life – foul language, dirty wellingtons, wife-swapping and after hours drinking.

Since that emaciated vileness, Tinniswood, wrote about me in a recent book, for which incidentally he paid me not one single penny, I have been inundated with requests to give more detailed information about my place of domicile.

I have always been most reluctant to do this.

However, recent events, which I shall presently relate, have forced upon me 'a change of heart'.

So with a certain amount of trepidation and in the spirit of those immortal words of that most celebrated master of the English language, Mr E. R. 'Elizabeth Regina' Dexter – 'here goes'.

The village of Witney Scrotum lies 'somewhere in England'.

I shall not identify its geographical location more precisely for fear of its being invaded by fleets of motor charabancs stuffed full of grinning Nips, square-headed Huns and foul-smelling Frogs with unshaven armpits.

I am not a prejudiced man, but I firmly believe that scum of this sort should be shot on sight or interned behind barbed wire for life on bread and water together with the hordes of lilac-haired, pre-pubescent, stoop-shouldered yobboes from nearby Keating New Town with their boils and their pimples and their filthy underclothes and work-shy parents driving Japanese cars the shape of over-sized pilchard tins and wasting the natural resources of our precious planet by gobbling up vast acres of forest land to provide paper on which to print the cricket reports of Mr Tony Lewis.

Where was I?

Ah yes – the village.

Suffice it to say that our village nestles in a gentle curve of that most exquisite of chalk streams, the Somerset Kitchen, sheltered from the harsh northerly gales by the rolling uplands of the Mendis Hills.

All around are rich woodlands of hanging oak, beech and chestnut and on the exposed escarpments grow the two varieties of rowan, athol and eric.

Lush water meadows leading to the coppice at Cowdrey's Bottom are the haunt of winter wildfowl –

red-crested tolchard, lindwall, wellard and common pridgeon.

Mother Nature's munificence is indeed boundless.

Every prospect pleases.

And, looking down on our village, totally dominating it from every angle, is the massive and magnificent bulk of the ancient earthwork of Botham's Gut, and carved into its chalk flanks are the badges of every single first class cricket county cut by dissident Yorkshire professionals imprisoned during the long and bitter Wars of the Sellars.

I have given a general picture of Witney Scrotum.

Now let us fill in the details.

By far the finest way to approach the village is by the old carters' route from Milton Abbas and Milton Arthur.

We cross the River Kitchen by the old stone packhorse bridge at Dredge's Elbow, and as we turn the corner by the old artesian Popplewells we find ourselves on the outskirts of the village of Witney Scrotum.

Pause awhile.

Do you see those low stone buildings to your left?

Once they were the home of the ancient gimblett and tremlett makers, but now, alas, with the disappearance of the old rural festivals of Toad-Skinning Thursday and Circumcision Saturday, there is no longer a need for their craft and only one of their breed now remains.

And he, poor chap, lives in somewhat reduced circumstances in Bournemouth eking out a precarious living with his circumciser's bradawl behind the ladies' heel bar at Marshall and Pocock's department store.

But let us wipe away our salty tears and continue our stroll through the village.

Above us the rooks caw hoarsely in the elms for all the world like a massed choir of Robin Jackmans appealing for lbw at Sabina Park.

On the roof of the golf ball museum we see a pied wagtail flicking its tail and bobbing its head, constantly fidgeting, forever twitching, an avian Derek Randall, looking down into the yard of Fearnley's Mill, where the village senior citizens are happily working in the gentle sunlight on the latest batch of thatched space invader machines.

Move on, dear reader, move on.

Tread softly past the wrought iron gates of Squire Brearley's Queen Anne mansion, for we do not wish to disturb that gentle, kindly old scholar as he works on the eleventh volume of his masterpiece, 'A Treatise on the Surrey Philosophers, Hobbs and Lock, including an Analysis of their Influence on the Leg Spin Theory of the Middlesex and England philosopher, J. A. Jung, with particular reference to Lord Eric Russell's *A History of Western Philosophy* and its Impact on Wittgenstein's analysis of the laws of cricket entitled "A battle against the bewitchment of our intelligence by means of language".'

A soft word and friendly greeting to our lovable and harmless village idiot, old Ben Stansgate, and here we are in the centre of Witney Scrotum.

Do you see?

There facing each other across the square are those twin bastions of village life, the pub and the church.

Look.

Sitting on a bench outside the Baxter Arms supping scrumpy and linseed oil shandies and drowsing in the sunshine are the venerable village elders Messrs Arlott, Mosey, Frindall and Alston, endlessly yarning about old campaigns in India, Australia, South Africa and the deathless, arid prose plains of British South West Dexterland.

They raise their forelocks to us as we leave them to their dreams and cross the square to the church.

What an exquisite Saxon edifice.

Clean and pure of line like a cover drive by Peter May.

Sturdy and honest like an over bowled by David Brown.

Chaste and virginal like an anecdote told by Barry Wood.

And inside the church displayed in a place of honour by the statuette of St Kevin de Keegan, the patron saint of endorsements, is one of our village's most cherished possessions.

It is, of course, a relic of the Blessed St Tony Greig of the Sorrows – a fragment of his money belt torn from his person during the Exodus From Sussex and lovingly restored by the master craftsman, Sebastian Coe, for a fee of £97,000, that being the cost of his second-class train fare from Sheffield.

Let us walk through the churchyard with its gravestones standing splintered and askew, its brooding yews and its monument to those brave village lads who fell in battle over countless centuries with its simple and moving inscription: 'Died of Drink'.

Let us rest our arms on the old moss-covered stone wall and gaze in peace and tranquillity at the pride and joy of Witney Scrotum – its cricket ground.

There stands the pavilion, timbered and hunched.

There stands the scorebox, tarpaulined and hushed.

There stands the groundsman, sullen and sloshed.

But wait.

Look at the pitch.

Dear God, it is scarred and criss-crossed with mounds of newly dug earth.

Have vandals been at work?

Have extremists carved into the turf of the wicket those dreaded words:

'Robin Marlar Is Innocent OK.'

No, my friends, that is not the case.

Relax, and I shall now relate my tale.

It starts in the early days of the present season when a small ridge appeared in the pitch just short of a length at the hoof warehouse end.

As the weeks progressed so did the ridge increase in size.

The members of our team, and, indeed our opponents, too, were content to accept it as one of the many natural hazards which add such spice and excitement to our beloved 'summer game' – exploding tea urns, infected egg and cress sandwiches, lady wives with loathsome unmarried sisters in Cheltenham and confounded Bedlington terriers constantly scratching and flecking and burying apostle teaspoons in the commodore's herbaceous border.

I am not a prejudiced man, but . . .

Where was I?

Ah yes, the ridge.

It was our village blacksmith, Gooch, who discovered

the true nature of the protruberance, and thus earned for himself a place of honour in cricket's 'hall of fame'.

He was batting against our visitors, a Michael Parkinson Invitation XI, which curiously enough included neither David Niven nor Billy Connolly, when a fastish away swinger delivered by their opening bowler, Mr Sammy Kahn, father of the former Pakistani Test cricketer, Majid, struck the ridge and, flying upwards and inwards, struck him a fearful blow on the left temple.

In a rage Gooch, normally the mildest of men, thrashed out with his bat at the offending ridge.

Soon turf and earth were flying in every direction.

And then of a sudden there was a loud metallic clank.

Gooch stopped dead in his tracks.

He knelt down and produced from the depths of the crater he had made with his bat a battered, rusting metal cask.

Our stumper, the village sub-post master and accredited poacher, Prodger, took out from his hip pocket the oyster knife he habitually used for prising open the registered letters addressed to old Grannie Swanton, and, grinding his dentures most fearsomely, unlocked the cask.

An amazing sight met our eyes.

There glinting in the bottom of the cask were six small irregular-shaped metal objects.

What were they?

Were they Mr Barry Wood's missing front teeth?

No.

It was old Squire Brearley, who with a stroke of pure genius, guessed their true identity.

'They are primitive Iron Age coins,' he said.

'And there are six of them. Six? Don't you realize the significance of this?'

We shook our heads.

Squire Brearley tugged his grizzled, shag pile beard and smiled.

'It is obvious,' he said.

'Six coins.

'Who uses six coins?

'Of course, my friends, of course.

'They are the coins used by some ancient umpire to count the number of balls bowled in some ancient over during some ancient and hitherto unknown cricketing culture.'

We gasped with admiration.

We threw up our hats in the air.

Strong men wept.

Poor old doddery Mosey spilled a jug of prime Cliff and Bradley Lancashire Exhibition bitter down the front of his moleskin romper suit.

Dear Lord, we had made history.

When news of our discovery reached 'headquarters', the duty flying squad detachment from MCC's stand-by archaeologists' unit was instantly dispatched to our ground to commence a 'dig'.

Hence, dear readers, the scars on the pitch.

Hence the mounds of earth.

Hence the unrestrained jubilation in our village, for here at Witney Scrotum we had discovered a previously unknown primitive culture to rank alongside those of the Beaker People, the Windmill Hill Folk and the Wombwell Cricket Lovers' Society.

And what treasures were brought up from the bowels of the earth.

Let me list just a few:

Two fossilized score card printing presses and a pair of stumper's gloves made from flint.

The earliest known biography of Sir Geoffrey Boycott.

Ornate bronze brooches bearing mottoes such as 'Botham Is King' and 'Tony Lewis for Grandstand'.

An early pottery pavilion gents urinal stall still blocked by the original filter tip cigarette butts.

Jockstraps made from a primitive form of tupperware and sellotape, thus proving, what had long been suspected, that even in those distant times men were in possession of what we now know as 'private parts'.

We know little of the lives of these people.

From remains of food examined in a charnel pit we can deduce that even during the Iron Age cricketers were eating potted meat sandwiches and angels on horseback.

From motifs on their pottery artefacts we know that, as now takes place with losing Australian Test captains, human sacrifice was resorted to in times of crisis.

But the most important discovery concerned their method of burial, and from this is derived their name in the archaeological canon.

It was towards the end of the dig that a long barrow was discovered in the region of deep third man just short of the groundsman's underground whisky still.

When it was painstakingly and carefully uncovered, there were revealed rows and rows of human skeletons laid out feet first in individual leather containers with primitive handles on either side.

And thus they are now known to scholars as the Cricket Bag People.

Speaking for myself entirely personally, there is only one thing which marred the pleasure of this discovery.

When the skulls of these people were taken to London and scientists set to work on them to reconstruct their facial appearance, it was revealed that every one of them without a single exception looked exactly like one man and one man alone.

Yes, dear readers, you have guessed.

It was Mr H. D. 'Dicky' Bird.

I am not a prejudiced man, but. . .

15
The Boys of Summer

The winter sun filters shyly through the shrouds of mist that hush the water meadows by Cowdrey's Bottom.

The wing beat of swan, the yackle of woodpecker, the scrawk of gull, the crunch of wellington boots on new-dropped snow – I am at ease, dear readers.

The lady wife lies confined to her bed with bedsock poisoning.

I am content.

Her loathsome unmarried sister is safely snowed up in Cheltenham.

I am.at peace with the world.

What did the poet say?

Clear the air!
Clean the sky!
Wash the wind!
Take stone from stone and wash them.

Bloody fool.

None the less, it confirms what I have always steadfastly maintained throughout all the many vicissitudes which life has thrown in my way – monsoons in the Bay of Bengal, typhoons in Tahiti, confounded Bedlington terriers snapping at one's ankles en route to the ablutions offices in the bleak watches of the night.

My belief is this:

The association between men of letters and practitioners of the 'summer game' has been long and felicitous and has enriched and ennobled every strand in the weft and the warp of our way of life.

The poet I have just quoted, for example, is Mr T. S. Eliot.

And he, of course, achieved even wider fame as the brother of the Derbyshire cricketer and Test umpire, Charlie.

Indeed, as I pen these lines, there are playing currently in the first class game several of our most distinguished 'literary lions'.

I think of Gloucestershire's Brian Brain, author of *Room at the Top*, of Denis Amiss and his hilarious rib-tickler, *Lucky Jim*, of Yorkshire's David Bairstow and his moving and sensitive *A Kind of Loving*, and, of course, the delicious Mr P. 'Beryl' Bainbridge of Gloucestershire, author of *The Bottle Factory Outing*, the mirthquaking account of the annual waysgoose of the Professional Cricketers' Association.

In addition to these celebrated novelists we find playing for Northamptonshire the distinguished poet and philosopher, Wayne Larkins, while Lancashire are lucky enough to have on their staff that amusing and witty *Guardian* cartoonist, Jack 'Posy' Simmons.

Incidentally is it not somehow comforting and appropriate that the current 'skippers' of the 1981 England rugby union football and cricket teams are named respectively Beaumont and Fletcher?

I await in a fever of excitement for the day when the captains of our national ladies netball and rugby league sides are named respectively Sherrin and Brahms.

However, it is not all 'one-way' traffic.

The literary history of the western world is full of examples of highly esteemed writers plying their craft on subjects dear to our beloved 'summer game'.

I think immediately in this context of Samuel Beckett, author of the controversial and deeply influential, *Waiting for Boycott.*

But how many of you, dear readers, know of two equally stimulating masterpieces which come from the pen of this well-loved 'Broth of a Boy'?

Grossly neglected, I feel, is his surrealistic novel about a long, damp and wicketless afternoon in the life of an Australian fast bowler playing for Lancashire, entitled *Malone Dies.*

And I can recommend without reservation the same author's brilliant playlet about the final years in the career of a Gloucestershire and England batsman, entitled *Crapp's Last Tape.*

Another writer who has ventured into the 'genre' is

Mr Len Deighton, better known perhaps as the author of a series of dazzlingly witty and inventive spy novels.

Without hesitation I would bestow the sobriquet 'a minor masterpiece' on *Bomber*, his biography of the Gloucestershire and Nottinghamshire spinner, Mr B. D. Wells.

Although Mr Deighton would, I am sure, be the first to pay tribute to the 'inside knowledge' of the subject he received from his father, the former Lancashire and Army cricketer, Captain J. H. G. Deighton.

Let us venture further into our examination of the subject.

The list of writers is indeed extensive.

It includes, among many others:

Thomas Armstrong and his biography of an extremely small Lancashire batsman, *Pilling Always Pays*.

Captain W. E. Johns, creator of the immortal Biggles, and his superb adventure yarns, *Gimblett Mops Up* and *Worrell Scores A Ton*.

Edna O'Brien's finely-constructed chronicle of family life in successive generations of an Essex county team, *The Casualties of Pearce*.

I much admire Evelyn Waugh's savagely satirical bowlers' coaching manual entitled *Put Out More Faggs*, and his affectionate monograph on Mr Robin Marlar, *The Loved One*.

The moving television screen has also provided a masterpiece in Mr Jeremy Sandford's tear-jerker set on the practice ground at Headingley and called *Athey Come Home*.

And the world of classic literature has produced a colossus in the shape of Mr D. H. 'Sid' Lawrence's epic story of a Surrey fast bowler, entitled *Sons and Govers*.

Dear Lord above, even the Americans have got into the act.

Who can ever forget Ernest Hemingway's masterly account of Mr Ian Botham's hitting exploits in the recent Test series against Australia, *Across the River and into the Trees*, and his sensitive and generous tribute on the retirement from the first-class game of Kent's most distinguished wicket keeper/batsman, entitled *A Farewell to Ames*.

You may wonder, dear readers, from whence I have acquired this extensive knowledge.

Well, literature has been a life-long interest of mine, along with cigarette cards, train-spotting, indoor yodelling, amateur fretwork, vintage Vimto, ancient bannisters and the incidence of litotes in the collected works of Lord Henry Blofield.

Indeed in my study now lying under the supine body of the cat are several priceless manuscripts which their famous authors have hitherto refused to publish.

Let us cuff the cat round the ear, and, giving him a thorough thrashing with a six-inch ruler, remove the manuscripts and examine them more closely.

This one, for example:

An extract of a play written by Mr Harold Pinter, brother of the former Burnley and England centre forward, Ray.

It is entitled *The Umpire*.

ACT ONE: SCENE ONE

A CRICKET GROUND. A MATCH IS TAKING PLACE. IT IS A MINOR COUNTIES MATCH. IT IS

BETWEEN KENT SECONDS AND HERTFORDSHIRE. A BATSMAN WALKS SLOWLY TO THE WICKET. THE UMPIRE AT THE BOWLER'S END WATCHES HIM SILENTLY AS HE PLACES HIS BAT CAREFULLY INTO THE CREASE AND SLOWLY RAISES TWO FINGERS.

BATSMAN: Middle and leg.

[PAUSE]

UMPIRE: I shouldn't be standing at Sidcup.

[PAUSE]

I should be standing at Lords.

[PAUSE]

I got my papers at Lords.
If only the weather would break, I'd be able to get to Lords.

[PAUSE]

What did you say?

BATSMAN: Middle and leg.

[PAUSE]

UMPIRE: You see, what it is, you see, I changed my name.
Years ago.
I been going around under an assumed name.
D. O. Oslear's not my real name.
No.
Not by any stretch of the imagination

[PAUSE]

Were you wanting something?

BATSMAN: Middle and leg.

[PAUSE]

UMPIRE: Spencer.
Tom Spencer.
That's my name.
That's the name I'm known by, anyway, when I'm standing at Sidcup.

[PAUSE]

When I'm standing at Maidstone it's Aspinall.
Ron Aspinall.

[PAUSE]

Nice name, Ron.

[PAUSE]

What was it you were wanting?
BATSMAN: Middle and leg.
UMPIRE: It's the shoes, you see.
I can't go to Lords in these shoes.
Last time I went to Lords in these shoes I seen the President, name of Brown.
F. R. Brown.
I said, you haven't got a pair of shoes, have you? I heard you got a stock of shoes here, I said.
'Piss off,' he said.

[PAUSE]

You were saying?
BATSMAN: Middle and leg.

[PAUSE]

UMPIRE: Piss off.

In that extract the part of the umpire was played by Miss Constant Cummings.

The batsman was played by Dame Derek Evans of Glamorgan.

The identity of the author of the next manuscript to be examined might surprise some lovers of the 'summer game'.

She is none other than Miss Barbara Cartland who in recent years has achieved national fame for her appearances on the moving television screen, bellowing in stentorian tones:

'Sit!'

However, there is another side to this talented creature.

Her deep, innate modesty and intense shyness have tended to obscure the fact that she is a writer of no little distinction in the field of romantic fiction.

Her novels, written with intense artistic integrity and awesome fastidious diligence to the minutest detail of character, plot and dialogue at the rate of one every two hours, have brought her a small but loyal following among retired colonels of the Royal Army Dental Corps, middle-aged shop assistants on the bacon counter of Tesco's Foodstores and fast bowlers confined to the ablutions offices during MCC tours to India and Ceylon.

It is high time her works reached a wider audience and with this end in view I am happy to present an extract from her enchanting novelette, *Bowling the Maiden Over*.

She stood there on the greensward at Brighton.

Brighton! Here the regency bucks and dandies had conducted their dalliances with the fashionable courtesans of high society.

Brighton! Here the bright young things of the twenties had come for passionate weekends of chaste romance under a sickle moon with the gentle waft of scented sea breezes whispering to them the poetry of love.

Brighton! Would they ever really establish themselves in the First Division of the Football League?

Her reveries were interrupted as a ripple of applause rippled among the spectators whose honest ruddy faces rippled the splintered summer sunlight.

She looked up and her heart missed a beat.

It was him.

No.

It was he.

He strode out to the wicket with that lissom lilt to the limbs, that purposeful manly tread, that ripple of rippling muscles that turned her knees to jelly.

And how her heart fluttered to the jut of his jaw, the straightness of that aristocratic aquiline nose, the haughty glint to those broodingly passionate smouldering eyes that rippled beneath the rippling black of his noble mane.

'Dexter, Dexter,' she breathed to herself.

Now she could feel the juices quicken in her body as he approached the wicket.

Nearer and nearer and nearer he came and then of a sudden he was standing next to her.

In person.

What would he say if he knew that it was her – no, it was she – who was standing at the bowler's end disguised as the celebrated umpire and mobile hat stand, Mr H. D. 'Dicky' Bird?

She was soon to have the answer.

Flexing his arms and rippling the muscles of his jaw he turned to her and said:

'Whatho, Dicky. How are the old piles this morning?'

At that moment something in her snapped.

The floodgates burst open and torrents of passion engulfed

her soul and in a blind ecstasy of rippling sensuousness she flung herself at her beloved bringing him crashing to earth just short of a length at the batsman's end.

'Dexter, Dexter,' she cried as she smothered his face with a passionate ripple of kisses and tore with feverish fingers at his cravat and his Gunn and Moore waterproof boil plasters.

'What the devil are you doing, Bird?' bellowed the manly rippling voice of the precious being around who – no, around whom – her whole existence revolved.

'I love you, I love you,' she gasped.

'Oh, God,' he said, 'it's Arthur Jepson all over again.'

Thus it was three weeks later she found herself at Lords sitting in front of the disciplinary committee composed of some of the highest dignitaries in the 'summer game'.

But the words they spoke made only a rippling drone in the back of her fevered mind.

She had eyes for only one man.

He sat facing her, slowly munching a Bounty Bar.

Their eyes met, and she felt a ripple of animal passion pass between them.

Oh, the sensuous lilt to his lips. Oh, the proud and noble tilt to his head. Oh, the ripples of passion in his eyes.

'Bedser, Bedser,' she whispered to herself.

Finally I have a task of honour to perform.

Duty compels me to put right one of the greatest acts of calumny ever perpetrated against our greatest poet of the 'summer game'.

I refer, of course, to Mr Dylan Thomas, known throughout the world as 'Wales's answer to Mr Wynford Vaughan Thomas'.

I have before me the manuscript of his majestic poem, 'I see the boys of summer in their ruin.'

It is this work which has been the object of such vileness.

There are certain long-haired, damp-fingered nancy boys with scent-laden armpits, who, posing as critics and arbiters of public taste, claim that the subject matter of this poem is what Lord Baden-Powell called in a moment of genius 'beastliness'.

Could anything be more damaging to a man's reputation than an accusation of such baseness?

Viler still, could anything be more designed to cast dark shadows on the characters of the countless millions of virtuous, virginal young men who have played our dear 'summer game'?

Let us look at the first verse of this superb poem and scotch forever this wicked accusation.

> I see the boys of summer in their ruin
> Lay the gold tithings barren
> Setting no store by harvest, freeze the soils;
> There in their heat the winter floods.
> Of frozen loves they fetch their girls,
> And drown the cargoed apples in their tides.

Good God, the meaning is clear enough.

It is this:

'The boys of summer' are those honest, hard-working, journeymen county cricketers, who, knowing they have no chance of making the MCC winter touring party, go out in the last match of the season to have a damn good joyous slog 'setting no store by harvest' of a decent score and looking forward to a winter spent with lady wives and sweethearts quaffing vast quantities of cider by drowning 'the cargoed apples in their tides'.

Could anything be plainer than that, dear readers?

These pomaded, simpering, limp-wristed homos with their disgusting sexual proclivities – how dare they impute that the flower of our cricketing manhood with their long, slim fingers entwining rich and silky balls and their firm fresh hands sliding slowly up and down quivering erect bat handles could ever have been guilty of 'beastliness'?

I rest my case.

16
Batman

The summer of '81.

What a vintage season.

What deeds of derring-do.

Such excitements, such tensions, such dramas.

It will live forever in the memories of all lovers of our blessed 'summer game'.

In Witney Scrotum, too, we had 'our moments'.

The white admirals returned to my garden for the first time in fifteen years.

The auxiliary fire brigade was called out three times to deal with conflagrations in the copse at Cowdrey's Bottom.

And, most blissful of all, for seven solid weeks the lady wife's confounded Bedlington terriers were laid low with a bout of canine piles.

But these, of course, are the musings of a 'village Hampden'.

Enough of nonentities.

Let us concentrate on that one man who strode through the season like a colossus, who thrilled us, who inspired us, who made strong men weep tears of joy, who sent surges of long-lost patriotic fervour coursing through the veins of every man, woman and child in this dear country of ours, who excited the immortal Mr E. R. 'Elizabeth Regina' Dexter to dizzy heights of sublime prose, which even he in his eminence could scarcely have hoped to attain.

I quote:

'He played a real "snorter" of an innings.'

Such command of language.

Such beauty of style.

And to whom was he referring?

Of course, dear readers, of course.

He was referring to that most celebrated son of Botham City – Batman.

There now – the secret is out.

I was sworn to secrecy, I confess, but after sleepless nights of torment and torture wrestling with my conscience, I have reached the conclusion that it is my duty, despite prior reassurances, to reveal the truth, the whole truth and nothing but the truth to the nation at large.

So – to use another of Mr E. R. 'Elizabeth Regina' Dexter's memorable phrases – 'here goes'.

Botham City, the home town of our hero of the

summer of '81, is more widely known to you and me, dear readers, as Keating New Town.

Keating New Town – what a sad, dismal testimony to all that is base and vile in contemporary society.

It was built with such high hopes.

Yes, it was a noble ideal to provide a new town in the heart of the English countryside for the poor wretches from the slums of our loathsome industrial cities.

But dear God, was it necessary to build the bloody thing a mere spit and a Honda ride away from Witney Scrotum?

The execrable selfishness of town planners, architects, local councillors, members of Parliament and similar scum is totally beyond comprehension.

There are times on summer Sunday evenings when it seems that the whole of Witney Scrotum is under siege by moronic louts riding oversized electric razors, picking their revolting ape-like noses with nicotine-stained fingers the size and shape of frost-bitten parsnips, and all of whom appear to be called Wayne or Darren.

I am not a prejudiced man, but when I think of rabble of this sort using up the precious oxygen of this dear planet of ours to fill up their soot-clinkered lungs in order to give them the strength to suck on their limp home-rolled cigarettes and to ceaselessly and publicly scratch their private parts, around which the whole of their nauseating existences revolve, I am filled with . . .

No, dear readers, no.

I shall contain myself.

I shall concentrate my attentions on 'the hero of the hour' – Batman of Botham City.

Let me conduct you to his place of abode.

Come with me to Keating New Town, and let us search out our hero 'in situ'.

We stand for a moment in the main square of the town, the Grand Place Hetherington, situated on the site of the ancient Grauniad Abbey.

The Grand Place Hetherington – what a pathetic hulk it now is.

Unemployment, vandalism and simple 'bad planning' have reduced this once proud public monument to a broken-down shambles.

Boarded up now are the grog shops, the wine bars, the taverns, the pubs, the open-air cafés, which gave it such gaiety and animation in the days of its prime.

It stands now eerie and deserted, bewildered and defeated by the brutal hands of fate.

Let us wipe away our tears and, turning our backs on this old ruin, hurry away down Billington Avenue.

Here, too we are faced with desolation and despair.

What folly to have expected the sub-human louts from the loathsome industrial cities with their luminous socks and their bulbous wristwatches to respond to the cultural offerings of the Harris-tweeded, limp bow-tied weirdos and nancy boys from the Arts Council and the St John Stevas Academy of Woodcraft and Rock Climbing.

Just look.

The Dame Sybil Thornber Memorial Theatre is an empty shell.

The De Jongh Theatre of the Absurd is a rotting hulk, cruelly defaced by graffiti, most of it in the handwriting of Brian Chugg, L. P. Samuels and Enid J. Wilson.

And, saddest of all, the building which housed the Jill

Tweedie Feminist Consort Fully Committed Parabolic Circus is now used as a mail order warehouse for the sale of novelty condoms, Polly Toynbee naughty flannelette nighties and Katie Stewart erotic cricket pads.

We carry on down Billington Avenue, and shortly we arrive at the Peter Jenkins Industrial Estate.

What a wasteland of unfulfilled promise and thwarted expectations.

Do we blame the planners once more?

In this case I think not.

Who could possibly have forecast all those years ago that there would be such a dramatic and catastrophic collapse in the British stapling machine industry?

Who could have predicted the world-wide slump in demand for bakelite shoe horns and non-stick underpants?

Who could have foreseen the havoc the Japanese would play among our traditional export markets in odourless fly-paper, tungsten pumice stone holders and musical bulldog clips?

Now the factories which housed these enterprises lie still and silent, and over all of Keating New Town there hangs the ghastly spectre of unemployment, poverty and the television reviews of Miss Nancy Banks-Smith.

Let us hurry away, for now we are within reach of our hero.

Turn the corner into Lacey Close.

Cut through the snicket into Rodda Drive and there in front of us is his place of residence.

Here is the shrine to which cricket lovers from all over the country will soon come to worship, if I reveal its identity.

Shall I?

Shall I, shall I?

Yes.

Yes, I owe it to you, dear readers.

The abode of Batman of Botham City, the hero of the summer of '81, is a corner shop.

And above the window written in letters of lime green and modest size is the legend:

'Neville Gribley – Wavy Line Grocer.'

I hear the gasps of horror.

The shock waves reverberate from every part of the country and shake my priceless collection of miniature cricket balls here in my study at Witney Scrotum.

Batman a grocer?

The man who single-handedly won two Test Matches for England against Australia is a purveyor of baked beans, Meltonian shoe polish and special offer toilet rolls?

Yes, 'tis so, dear readers, 'tis so.

Press your nose against the window of the shop and look inside.

Yes.

There he is.

That man in the nigger brown cardigan, the baggy chalk-stripe flannels and the grease-scuffed Hush Puppies reaching up for a packet of sultanas is indeed Batman.

Now do you understand?

It is only in moments of greatest national emergency that he rips off his Aertex singlet, his clip-on St Michael bow tie and surgical sandals and dons the uniform of Batman – the pristine white sweater under which bulges the noble barrel chest, the snow-white flannels under which ripple those whipcord muscles, the navy-blue war helmet and the false beard from the Alec and Eric Bedser Tee Hee Joke Shop.

At all other times Batman is simple Neville Gribley, five foot three in his stocking feet, seven and a half stone (excluding the three ball point pens and seven propelling pencils he carries constantly on his person) and a man of profound meekness, sensitivity and modesty.

The 'real' Batman, the 'real' hero of the summer of '81, is a simple soul frightened of mice and cockatiels, totally opposed to strong drink and bold women, a devotee of 'Crossroads' and the works of O. S. Nock, a man whose principal pleasure is indoor embroidery and the restoration of vintage bicycle pumps.

Let us enter the shop.

The bell jingles merrily.

We listen to his soft and diffident voice as he speaks to his customers.

'Yes, Mrs Gower, we do have a special offer in hair nets this week. Very reasonable, and if you buy six, you get a free oven pad.'

'Hello, Mrs Fletcher, love. You're looking down in the dumps again. Why don't you try the gregory powder this week instead of the Ex-Lax?'

'Morning, Mr Gatting. No we don't stock those. I'd try the barber, if I was you.'

Let us creep past him and enter his private quarters.

How neat. How tidy. How fastidious.

In his diner/kitchenette everything is spotless.

The tupperware gleams. The teatowels are starched snowy white. The muslin covers on the marmalade jars are immaculate. And there is not a single stain on his tin of Bournvita.

And upstairs in his dear little bedroom with its Clara Cluck frieze his night attire is neatly folded in his Mike Brearley autograph pyjama case, there is not a speck of wax in his nightlight holder and his Hobbs and Sutcliffe Teamaker stands proudly on his cane bedside table next to the silver-framed photo of Mr Ian Chappell.

And there under the window is a low bookcase.

Let us examine the books it contains, for these can reveal much about a man's nature.

There they are, still in their original dust jackets – the complete works of Catherine Cookson, a first edition of *Bunkle Buts In*, seven *Radio Fun* albums, three *Teddy Tail* annuals, seven volumes of Arthur Mee's guide to the counties of England and a paperback anthology of the best of the cricket reports of Mr Tony Lewis.

But, of course, it is 'the smallest room in the house' which is most indicative of his character.

How delicately he has embroidered his toilet roll covers.

How assiduously he has hoovered the drip mat and harpicked the bidet.

The whole establishment smells like a timid early morning glade in the heart of the New Forest, and far be it from me to destroy that pristine freshness after our lunch of lobster vindaloo, tarka dhal and home-brewed curried lager.

Let us descend the stairs and talk to our hero, for it is his evening break, and he is only too happy to share with us his pot of Mazawattee tea and his plate of custard creams

Let us allow him to 'speak for himself', shall we?

'Yes,' he says, as with crooked little finger he delicately dunks a biscuit in his willow pattern tea cup. 'Yes, I have got ambitions.

'My fondest ambition, i.e. what I'd like to do most in this world, is to own a knitting wool shop in Basingstoke.

'Or failing that I'd like to go half shares in a garden centre, concentrating mainly on the indoor pot plants.

'I seem to have an affinity with them. You should see my Busy Lizzy.'

Is he happy with his lot?

'Oh yes. Yes, indeed. You see, there's a lot to recommend this life.

'I think I'm providing what I call "a service to the community", which is not provided by the supermarkets with their impersonal service and their relative inaccessibility.

'And I do think I compete with them most favourably as regards prices, particularly on my bacon counter where I do a very good line in knuckles.

'You see, the nice thing about this job is that you become what I like to call "a member of the community".

'For instance, I'm always ready to break off serving to have a chat and a natter with one of my "young mums" or help my senior citizens over the road if they're "unsteady on their pins".

'The things I hear sometimes. Honestly!'

And what about his social life?

'Well, basically, I am a rather shy and reticent person once out of the environs of the shop.

'I used to like going to the cinema until they started showing rude films.

'And I used to go every Friday to the public baths until they converted it to mixed bathing.

'Basically, though, I'm what I like to call "a home-loving person".

'I like watching "Crossroads" on the telly – isn't it scandalous what they did to Meg Richardson? – and I have to confess I'm rather fond of "Blankety Blank", particularly when they have Kenny Everett on it. Isn't he a yell?

'I like "Give Us a Clue", too, although I do wish Michael Aspel would tell us sooner when they're going to put the clue up on the screen.

'In the main, however, I prefer what I like to call "the wireless".

'I like Ken Ford on "Gardeners' Question Time" – hasn't he got a deep manly voice? – and I'm a great fan of Louise Botting on "The Money Programme".

'Also I like "Yesterday in Parliament", the Legal Beagle on the Jimmy Young Show and any programme that deals with our "feathered friends".'

And what about romance?

Is there a little lady in his life?

'Oh no.

'You see, basically, I'm very shy as regards what I like to call "the opposite you-know-what".

'As I never drink anything stronger than Vimto, I never go to public houses, and that's where you meet young ladies these days, isn't it?

'Mind you, I do dream about them sometimes.

'I have this dream which I have quite often actually.

'There's these young ladies and they're wearing nothing but cricket caps and they're heaving and straining and pulling the heavy roller at Taunton and they're being whipped by Vivian Richards who's wearing nothing but a gold lamé jock strap and they've painted his nipples carmine and his buttocks are. . .'

At this moment there is a strident buzz on the telephone.

It glows, and it pulsates.

Our hero leaps up from his uncut moquette Waring and Gillow granny rocker and wrenches up the receiver.

'Yes, yes, yes,' he says tersely.

He slams down the receiver.

Gerrow.

Zak.

Yoweee.

Tcherooooooooooooooo.

In an instant he is transformed into Batman.

The chest bulges.

The muscles ripple.

He raises his bat to his shoulder.

He adjusts his abdominal protector.

And:

Gerrow.

Zak.

Yoweee.

Tcherooooooooooooooo.

In a screech of tyres and a deep-bellied snarl of jet engine he disappears from our view in his blood red Bothamobile.

Yes, Batman is off again to do battle for Queen and country.

Whither is he bound?

To knock the stuffing out of Indian spin bowlers?

To thrash the living daylights out of Mr H. D. 'Dicky' Bird?

To liberate Afghanistan from its Russian overlords and free Tibet from the yoke of Chinese oppression?

Maybe.

It is, however, my personal hope that he is off to Westminster to give a severe ear-cuffing to that slimy little shit, Mr Leo Brittan.

However, all in good time we shall know the purpose of his mission.

Let us leave now.

One moment.

The lady wife sent me on an errand for a packet of marzipan paste.

There it is on the shelf next to the tins of pilchards and the packets of bi-carb.

No, dear readers, I have not forgotten.

I have left the money on the counter.

Dear God, we don't want a visit from Batman in Witney Scrotum.

17
Five Non-Cricketers

It is a fact totally beyond dispute that one of the greatest and noblest joys of summer for men of 'cricketing bent' is that wondrous and precious moment when the lady wife scoops up her confounded Bedlington terriers and encamps for Cheltenham to spend three weeks with her loathsome unmarried sister.

Peace and serenity.

The lady wife is gone, and the sun shines stronger in the heavens, the birds sing sweeter in the meadows, the whisky glows tangier in the decanters, and a chap can go to bed secure in the knowledge that his nocturnal ablutions activities will not be irretrievably soured each time he returns to the bedroom by his lady wife barking in that hideous hectoring voice:

'I hope you've shaken your Thing properly.'

Dear readers, is there any greater joy known to man than the slow pad-padding through the rooms of a house shorn of the odious omniscient presence of its mistress?

The very fabric of the building seems to croon with contentment.

The dust gathers softly on the bookshelves like dandruff on the collar of a Surrey blazer, shreds of burning tobacco float gently down to the china rug like the acrid smuts of Leeds floating down to the wicket at Headingley, and the cooker top grows greasier and greasier for all the world like the hair of the young Denis Compton.

There are moments to savour.

For now a man may indulge in those forbidden pleasures of the flesh, which so outrage the cruder sensibilities of the lady wife.

How perfect to stand at the open french windows of the drawing room on a fresh summer's morn and, by carefully extending the right leg sideway and raising the right foot three inches above the ground, slowly and rapturously break wind.

How sublime to abandon all furtiveness and with blithe abandon affix to the corner of the kitchen tablecloth the contents of one's left nostril.

How blissful to lie pink and soaking in a brimming bath with carnal thoughts of Mr K. D. 'Slasher' MacKay flickering through the mind, knowing that one's reverie will not be shattered rudely by the lady wife marching in with her hateful dipstick and declaring:

'You brute, there's more than three inches of hot water in this bath.'

It was with pleasurable anticipations such as these suffusing my whole being in a deep and rosy glow that I sped homewards in the trusty Lanchester after depositing the lady wife and her confounded Bedlington terriers with her nauseous pile of consanguinity at Cheltenham.

I knew of an inn where strong ale was dispensed in mellow old pewter tankards.

I knew of a wayside cottage where thick and sizzling gammon was served with orange-yoked eggs and plump, sizzling mushrooms, golden potato cakes and mugs of sweet brown tea.

I knew of a riverside hostelry whose landlord had once opened the batting for Minor Counties versus Pakistani Eaglets and whose scrumpy was the colour and consistency of Tony Cordle's bathwater.

And then it happened.

A sudden howling and screeching, a volley of staccato explosions for all the world like Mr Robin Jackman appealing for a catch behind the wicket at Port of Spain, and the infernal engine of the trusty Lanchester went dead.

In vain did I thrash the brute.

In vain did I curse it.

The beast stood silent and still at the side of the road, its chrome radiator grill sneering superciliously at me, like the hideous elongated smile on the face of the Chappell brothers.

I lashed out with the toe of my boot, and as I recoiled backwards, howling with pain, I caught a glimpse of a figure standing placidly at a garden gate.

Those features were familiar.

So was the dress – the Pierre Cardin crocodile skin smoking jacket, the cerise suede knickerbockers, the Russell and Hobbs electric doeskin sneakers.

Yes, it was Woodcock of *The Times*.

Dear old Bruce Woodcock – a friendly face in hostile climes, a broad shoulder to cry on, a certain provider of strong liquor and scrumptious victuals.

I was not disappointed.

He took me gently by the arm and led me inside his charming old house, the Curacy, named thus in honour of the Rev. J. K. Aitchison of Scotland and the present Archbishop of Canterbury, Dr Fred Rumsey.

And there as the evening shadows lengthened and herons returned to their roosts high in the shimmering elms we ate packet after packet of his home-made bilberry-flavoured crisps and quaffed glass after glass of his home-brewed jock strap wine.

How he yarned about old times – those epic scraps of his in the ring with Tami Mauriello and Lee Oma and those later epic scraps in the press box at Taunton with Mr Robin Marlar and his musical father, Gustav, as the assembled hacks struggled for possession of the single Bill Frindall patent portable scorer's commode.

Later still as he passed round his home-stilled Thermogene gin he showed me a selection of some of his most prized possessions.

Item after item was dropped to the floor or trampled underfoot as we took it in turns to lurch to the 'facilities' behind the Fay Weldon autographed sightscreen at the bottom of the garden.

By the time we cracked the seventh bottle of home-cured bunion ointment whisky I confess we were both slightly 'stinko', not to say totally obfuscated and hiccius-doccius.

Nonetheless when he withdrew from the deepest recesses of his 'treasure chest' the pride of his cricketing souvenirs and mementoes my senses were of an instant sharp and crystal clear.

It is not generally known, I suspect, that Bruce Woodcock, apart from being chief cricket correspondent and men's fashion editor of *The Times*, is also editor of *Wisden's Cricketers' Almanack*.

It is even less well known that while that august journal publishes annually its five cricketers of the year, it also has specially written, although not for publication, its five non-cricketers of the year.

It was a selection of these articles which dear old Bruce offered for my perusal.

I know he will not object to my sharing a few with you, dear readers, as at the moment I purloined them he was lying prostrate on the floor drinking large draughts of home-made lint juleep out of an extremely rare example of Dame Peter West's left dancing pump.

So here for your delectation are five Wisden Non Cricketers of the Year:

The Maharajah of Rutnagur

Rutnagur achieved distinction as being the fattest man ever to play first-class cricket.

In his prime he weighed in at 52 stone and was forced to play the majority of his innings seated in a reinforced pre-stressed concrete howdah.

In a memorable innings of 8 made in eleven hours while playing for Delhi against Madras Nude Bicyclists

Gymkhana he came to the wicket weighing 33 stone and when finally given out weighed 37 stone, this being the result of his having consumed during his occupation of the crease five prawn vindaloo, eight chicken dhansak with fried rice, eleven mutton tikka with bindi bhajee, two trunkfuls of spiced poppadoms, one plate of curried abdominal protector in cricket bag sauce and both the umpires.

He was forced to retire from the first-class game when, with his side requiring only one run to defeat Bengal State Vegetarian Laundries and Dry Cleaners and thus win the Ranji Trophy, his massive bulk stuck fast in the pavilion door on his way to the wicket and, despite the heroic efforts of seventeen bull elephants on heat to drag him clear remained firmly embedded in the structure of the building, thus enabling his opponents to claim victory as no other batsman of his side was able to reach the wicket.

He was finally released through a joint operation involving a platoon of Ghurka sappers, a battalion of the North West Frontier Mounted Artillery and a squadron of dive bombers from the Royal Indian Air Force.

Next day his body was stuffed with 65 tons of bombay duck and pilaw rice and is now used as the spare heavy roller on the ground of the Bombay Mutual Tango and Gentleman's Onanists Club.

Banks-Smith, 'Nancy'

The only woman ever to have kept wicket for Worcestershire.

Many judges are of the opinion that she could ultimately have represented her country, but for one crucial failing in her armoury – a relentless desire to be funny at all costs.

Selection committees were prepared to ignore the ugly, crab-like stance when batting and the staccato, stuttering, disorientated style when 'wearing the gloves'.

What they could not ignore was her lack of generosity to team-mate and opponent alike through her refusal to cease dispensing jokes of profound feebleness.

Died laughing at her own jokes during an episode of *Brideshead Revisited*.

Currently employed on the staff of the *Guardian*.

Yarwood, M. J. K.

'Mike', as he is universally known to friend and foe alike, achieved a 'bumper' year in the season 1980.

As J. A. Ormrod of Worcestershire he came twentieth in the first-class batting averages.

And as P. J. Hacker of Nottinghamshire he reached twelfth position in the national bowling averages.

He also umpired the Second Test match against Australia in the persons of D. O. Oslear (the well-known cricketing misprint) and Mr H. D. 'Dicky' Bird.

Stansgate Wedgwood-Benn, Anthony

Without any doubt 'Gaters' was the outstanding schoolboy and varsity cricketer of his generation.

An aristocrat among batsmen, a crown prince among bowlers, a fielder of peerless elegance, he towered like a golden-skinned Colossus above his contemporaries.

He was a true all-rounder in the noble traditions of

Fry, Studd and Spooner, for not only was he a natural sportsman, excelling at assocation football, high hurdles, Graeco-Roman wrestling, crown green bowls and three card brag, but he was also an oustanding scholar, winning at his school the Michael Foot gold medal for casuistry and engine spotting seven years running.

But it is as a cricketer that he achieved his most memorable successes.

Few who were present will forget the brilliance of the treble century he scored before lunch while playing for his school against a formidable TUC Young Professionals XI skippered by the astute and wily Clive 'Roly' Jenkins.

Witnesses still talk with bated breath of the deviousness of the spinners he sent down while taking all ten wickets against a Socialist Dissidents and Thespians XI featuring Judith Hart and Gerald Kaufman playing the front end and back end respectively of Mr Denis Healey.

A glittering future of rampant success seemed assured.

What went wrong?

Some say it was overweening ambition, a desire to captain England 'at all costs'.

In the opinion of this writer, however, this is totally false, for 'Gaters' was a natural leader and the honour he so desired would have come inevitably to him regardless of any special endeavours on his part.

No, this writer steadfastly maintains that the failure of 'Gaters' to achieve the highest of honours and successes could be put down to one simple fact – an unhealthy and totally destructive pre-occupation with the 'low life'.

If only he had stuck to 'his own kind'.

When he came down from the varsity, he had the whole world at his feet.

Surrey, Middlesex, Kent and Sussex clamoured for his services as skipper.

With his natural beauty and grace, his wit, his erudition, his aristocratic birthright, he could have 'had his pick' and made his mark in any sphere of human activity he cared to choose.

But what did he do?

He turned his back on the first class game.

He abandoned his family seat in the country and his stately town house in London, he threw away his doeskin jodphurs and his shantung MCC blazers and, donning flat cap, muffler and moleskin waistcoat, began playing league cricket in the north of England.

Why?

Some people say it was because he gained a vicarious excitement from associating with people so obviously inferior to him in every facet of life.

Some people maintain he fell under the malign influence of the seedy, balding Yorkshire professional, Scargill, who used him simply as a means of obtaining free elocution lessons.

Others claim that it was the inherent nobility and generosity and passion of his nature that drove him on a missionary crusade to the dourlands of the north to preach to the working classes his fervent belief that the cover drive, the late cut and the wristy leg glance were not the sole province of the upper classes.

But whatever his motives poor 'Gaters' never fitted in.

Try as he might (and his endeavours were indeed assiduous) he never mastered the behaviour patterns of his new-found colleagues in northern league cricket.

The slack jaw, the gormless glaze to the eyes, the mean slit to the mouth, the swift drag on a Park Drive dimp between overs 'stumped' him completely, and, being a naturally gifted fielder, he found it impossible to drop his aitches.

Within a few years the gaiety and abandon of his stroke play had been replaced by a dour forward prod.

The lissom grace of his fielding had been replaced by a stoop-shouldered plod on the boundary and a weary underarm lob to the keeper.

The bowling arm dropped lower and lower.

He was just 'going through the motions'.

Eventually in a moment of supreme humiliation he was dropped from the team and relegated to the humble duties of baggage master and scorer.

Poor 'Gaters'.

His tragedy was that he desperately wanted to be a 'Player', but breeding and background doomed him to be forever a 'Gentleman'.

Tinniswood, Peter
The ultimate non-cricketer.

Holder of the record Lancashire opening partnership of 567 with his partner, Winston Place.

18
Sibson

Like all lovers of our dear 'summer game' I am addicted to Taverner's fruit drops.

Thank God, I had the foresight to lay down sufficient quantities of the great vintage of 1956.

Now, sucking a particularly majestic green fruit drop (as always the finest of the vintage) I find my mind filling up with overpowering remembrances of times past.

And I grieve.

I grieve for the loss of those institutions, those people, those objects of everyday life, which gave this great country of ours its infinite superiority over the mass rabbles of non-cricket-playing dagos, wops, frogs, Huns and similar scum too ghastly to mention.

There are grave questions to be asked about our past, dear readers.

Whatever became of Felix Mendelssohn and his Hawaian Serenaders?

Where oh where are Kitty Bluett and Pearl Hackney?

Why the demise of plus fours, nosebags, tram conductors' mittens and Lancashire leg spinners?

Will there ever be another Fred Loads?

I confess without shame that as the years draw in on me inexorably with the bleak relentlessness of a Michael Parkinson interview, it is nostalgia which warms my old bones and lags my thin veins against the icy chills of contemporary life.

Admit it, dear readers, it is thus with you.

It is nostalgia, pure and simple, which keeps you sane in these hideous days of Colonel Swanton's Fried Kentucky Chicken, H. D. 'Dicky' Bird and his loathsome instant custard, Jimmy Hill, Nigel Smarmer-Stiff, Tony Gubba Row and his brother, Ramon, Reichsmarschal von Pickering and Feldwebel Vine, the Dowager Duchess of Took, Pamela Stevenson (how much better the world would have been had he stuck to wicket keeping with Hampshire) that vileness Tariq Ali, and his father, the umpire Bill, Dennis Lillee.

Dennis Lillee – dear Lord above!

Only this morning I read in my newspaper that this wretched man took up his stance at the wicket with a bat which contained in its splice a digital clock.

Digital clocks – dear Lord above!

To my untutored eyes it seems that everything we purchase these days contains a digital clock.

Where will it all end?

Shall we have the beastly contraptions on our jock-straps, our bicycle clips, our MCC membership cards, our. . .

But no. Let me calm myself.

Let me comfort myself in the secure and tender embrace of blessed nostalgia.

As I sit now in the fluff-bound study of my home in Witney Scrotum I see all around me the souvenirs of my past.

My beloved grandfather's death mask, the nostrils of which serve as most useful receptacles for my pipe cleaners and hedgehog reamer.

My even more beloved grandmother's yak-hide ear trumpet which terrorized so many of the literary eminences of the time who attended her celebrated 'salons' at her London residence, the Aspels.

It is reliably reported in the memoirs of Dame Peter West that my grandmother used this ferocious instrument to great effect during a violent and physical argument between the author of *Vanity Fair*, Harry Makepeace Thackeray, and Mrs Gaskell, author of the definitive biography of a beloved Lancashire cricket captain, *Cranston*.

But I own, it is the souvenirs of my late father which move me most.

There on the table next to my Uncle Fishlock's drip-dry polo sticks I have them laid out in a place of honour.

I particularly treasure three sets of his best drinking braces made from toughest Michelin tyre tread and special non-corrosive metal buckles, his magnetic hip flask, his indoor whisky still disguised as a bust of Charlie Smirke, and his portable kidney douche.

Dear, dear father; he it was who many many years ago instilled into me feelings for the theatre which I hold to this very day.

How can I describe those feelings?

How can I do justice to the loathing, the nausea and disgust I hold for the whole panoply of conceit, vainglory and arrogance supported by unseemly hordes of braggarts, self-publicists and pomaded pansies?

I except from these strictures, of course, the celebrated light comedian and chanteuse, Mr John Inman, brother of that fine Pakistani Test cricketer, Mr Inman Khan.

And that doyen of the English stage, Sir Alf Richardson, husband of the former proprietress of 'Crossroads', Meg, and father of the two cricketing brothers, Peter and Derek.

But back to my father and his abiding interest in all matters of a Thespian nature.

Apart from being Chief Inspector of Bicycles and Tandems to the East Bengal Mounted Customs and Excise Hussars my father also achieved considerable distinction as an amateur inventor.

He it was who invented the inflatable toothpick for the use of lifeboatmen.

He it was who invented the luminous arch support for the use of explorers during the perpetual darkness of the arctic winter – a device also used by opening batsmen during the perpetual darkness of Old Trafford Test Matches.

It was in his capacity as an inventor that my father first met that giant of the English stage, that female colossus, who charmed us, enchanted us and captured our hearts for more than six generations until she was 'put down' by humane killer in the outside toilets of the Garrick Club.

I refer, of course, to Mrs Chester Dromgoole.

Her beauty was unrivalled.

Her wit was unparagoned.

How well I remember seeing her as a young boy in that ripping farce, *Arsenal and Old Lace*.

Among the dazzling cast was the bewitching Miss Winifred Emery, mother of that most subtle and sensitive of English actors, Mr Dick Emery, who coined as a catchphrase a remark made by Sir Donald Bradman to Mr Harold Larwood during the infamous 'bodyline' series in Australia:

'Oooh, you are awful, but I like you.'

It was a few weeks after this theatrical event that my father was summoned to a weekend house party at the country residence of Mrs Chester Dromgoole to demonstrate to her his latest invention, the portable wig.

Mrs Dromgoole, always a fitness fanatic, had recently been playing the arduous part of Othello in Shakespeare's play of a very similar name.

In order to achieve maximum physical soundness she had taken to training with members of the Millwall Association Football Club.

Unfortunately the constant heading of a sodden football had caused an unsightly bald patch to appear on the crown of her pate, thus necessitating the intervention of my father and his latest cranial creation.

Mrs Dromgoole expressed herself delighted with the wig, which served the dual purpose of concealing her trichopathic deficiencies and providing a warm and comforting night bed for her beloved Boston terrier, named after Julius Caesar, who coined another of cricket's immortal catchphrases:

'Come two, Brute.'

My father never ceased to talk with affection and enthusiasm of the blissful four days he spent at the gracious stately home set in the heart of the green and rolling hills of rural England.

Dear old 'Weskers' – how right that it should now be one of our country's most treasured national monuments.

The company that weekend was dazzling.

Statesmen, diplomats, politicians, great soldiers, dukes and duchesses, BBC executives and their wives strolled along the gravelled paths, lingered in the sweet-smelling conservatories and gossiped on the fine-cropped lawns.

Over breakfast that first morning my father shared a table with those two eminent men of letters, Sir Sacha Distel, and his brother, Dame Edith.

Later on the same day my father played a game of shuttlecock and battledore against a certain Irishman by the name of Wilde, who was partnered by a typically oily, garlic-stinking Frenchman, name of Proust.

My father was partnered by Lord Kitchener.

The sodomites won.

The perfect weekend was marred for my father by only one thing – the presence of a Norwegian playwright, who had achieved a certain modest success in his own country as the author of the play *Piers Gynt*.

His name was, I believe, Sibson.

Sibson's gloomy mien, his dark brooding silences and

the shapeless, shabby raincoat he wore constantly despite the noble, blazing English sun cast a sullen blight on the company which was not to be assuaged despite Mrs Dromgoole's heroic efforts to entertain her guests with her far-famed impersonations of the Langridge brothers, James and John.

My father well remembered his first encounter with Sibson, who was seated at an exquisite rosewood and tupelo escritoire next to the sightscreens in the writing room.

'Whatho, Sibson,' said my father. 'Scribblin' again, eh?'

Sibson fixed my father with a pair of cold blue eyes and said:

'Sir, I am writing a play in which the heroine refuses to discover herself, and her conflicts and her tragedy are the results of this refusal.

'Longing for life and yet afraid of it, she refuses to admit this fear and convert the energy of her conflict into action.

'And so at the centre if the play will be a mind turning upon itself in a kind of vacuum.'

'I see,' said my father. 'And are you using washable ink in your fountain pen?'

Many years later my father saw this play, *Edna Gobbler* in the company of two of the most august members of the cricketing establishment, Mr H. D. G. Leveson-Gower and Sir Pelham 'Plum' Warner, creator among many other things of the immortal catchphrase:

'Mind my bike.'

During the second act Sir Pelham, who had found increasing difficulty accommodating his nether regions, clad as they were in cricket pads and abdominal protector, in the narrow confines of the orchestra stalls, said in a very loud voice:

'Who are all these bloody Norwegians anyway?'

'Sir,' said my father. 'One is a puisne judge. The other is a scholar engaged in the history of civilization. And the chap with the big nose is his wife.'

'Splendid pair of shoulders on her,' said Leveson-Gower. 'Wonder if she'd like to open the bowling for me at the next Scarborough Festival?'

And with that the gentle snores of two of the most distinguished administrators in the history of the 'summer game' echoed sweetly round the theatre.

They were disturbed only when some damn fool let off a pistol at the end of the play, thus causing Sir Pelham to spill half a box of orange-flavoured chocolate dragees down the front of his MCC blazer.

I mention this incident only to emphasize a point that has so often been overlooked by the so-called experts and self-appointed arbiters of public taste, with their vile socks and adenoidal snufflings – the overriding influence exercised by the game of cricket on the most momentous and significant movements in the history of the drama.

For example, it was during that weekend at the residence of Mrs Chester Dromgoole that Sibson conceived the central theme of his most famous play.

A lot of bosh and tommy rot has been spoken and written about this, and I intend to 'put the record straight' here and now.

The facts are these:

On the Sunday afternoon, as was customary at these

house parties, Mrs Dromgoole split her guests into two teams to take part in a game of cricket.

Sibson was nowhere to be found.

It was the obsequious, shifty-faced butler, Billington, who finally discovered him skulking in the attic dressed in shabby greatcoat, woollen gloves and a dirty, reddish-brown wig, thus bearing a marked resemblance to Mr Patrick Moore in his Sunday best.

On being summoned to Mrs Dromgoole's presence and informed of her desire that he take part in the cricket match, Sibson thew up his hands and cried:

'But, merciful God, one doesn't do that kind of thing.'

It took all the tact of my father's hostess to persuade him to don Free Foresters' cap and I Zingari sweater, although he jibbed at wearing cricket flannels, protesting:

'One should never put on one's best trousers to go out to battle for freedom and truth.'

On seeing him take a net with Dame Flora Hobson, and her sister, the eminent drama critic and unicyclist, Dame Harold, my father well understood Sibson's reluctance 'to chance his arm'.

For his aptitude for the game could be summed up in three well-chosen words:

'No bally good.'

The two teams were captained respectively by Field Marshall Hindenberg and Lady Violet Bonham-Carter, a noted 'purveyor' in her own right of top spinner and chinaman.

Sibson opened the batting for Lady Violet's side and with typical Scandinavian two-eyed stance faced the first ball delivered by the immortal Lord 'Rolf' Harris.

The noble Lord, bowling over the wicket, sent down a short-pitched ball which rose sharply from the pitch and struck Sibson flush in the groin.

Much was the merriment of the spectators as the melancholic father of all subsequent plays concerned with the inner experience of the individual and the assessment and revaluation of his past at some ultimate turning point of his soul's pilgrimage hopped round on one leg clutching his private parts.

When he had regained his breath, Sibson pointed feebly at Lord Harris and cried:

'Go round, Peer.'

This Lord Harris did, and, bowling round the wicket, struck Sibson a formidable blow on the right temple.

It was obvious by now to one and all that his Lordship was determined to humble and humiliate the Norwegian for the gloom and despondency he had caused to settle on the company in the previous days.

The third ball thudded most frightfully into Sibson's chest.

The fourth, a beamer, caused him to fling himself full length on the pitch.

The fifth knocked out his two front teeth and the sixth, the most perfect of yorkers, totally wrecked his castle beyond redemption.

Sibson had not troubled the scorer.

And as he stormed back to the pavilion swinging his bat angrily, muttering dark Scandinavian curses and grinding his remaining Nordic teeth, we realize now only too well the origin of his most celebrated of plays.

I refer, of course, to *The Wild Duck*.

Later he was to write a somewhat less distinguished

play about the family of a former Lancashire and England opening batsman, entitled *The Pullars of the Community*.

19
The Royal Wedding

Like all lovers of our beloved 'summer game' I found last year's Royal Wedding the most damnable and thundering nuisance.

It confirmed conclusively what I have always believed most fervently and passionately.

It is this:

Any sphere of human activity given the 'seal of approval' by the distaff side in the person of the lady wife and all the other long-haired, loud-voiced, hairy-legged fraternity with their things on the front of their chests and their twanging corsets and their rasping knickers and their confounded Bedlington terriers and their loathsome unmarried sisters in Cheltenham can only be regarded by civilized man and member of MCC alike as utterly vile and detestable.

Consider those enterprises which receive their approbation – hanky-panky, dusting, armpit-shaving, hectoring, setting mousetraps, wiping lavatory seats, cutting toenails, lighting fires, chopping wood, repairing greenhouse guttering, changing the plugs on the trusty Lanchester and, worst of all by far, going to weddings.

Dear Lord, it would not be so bad if they did not insist on their menfolk being present and taking an interest while they are indulging in these squalid and totally unnatural undertakings.

Even after all these years I still feel a deep and brooding resentment towards the lady wife who insisted on my being present at our wedding, despite my having warned her six months previously that on that very day I had a long-standing arrangement to attend the annual luncheon of our cricket touring club, the Ditherers, at the Dexter Arms, Langridge-on-Sea.

I told her I was prepared to compromise.

I made a firm promise that if I could spare the time from the Scarborough Cricket Week, I would make every endeavour to spend a few days in her company on our honeymoon.

But no.

She 'dug in her heels' and with typical female selfishness insisted on my making a personal appearance at our wedding in tickety-boo order, despite my presenting her with a doctor's note to the effect that I had a deep-seated allergy to spats.

In this context I am reminded of a dear friend of mine

talking in bleak and gloomy tones about the arrival of yet another of his detestable offsprings.

'Were you present at its birth?' inquired a mutual acquaintance and 'more than adequate' stumper.

'Good God, no,' replied my friend. 'It was bad enough being present at its conception.'

This observation represents precisely my feelings on being compelled through the medium of the moving television screen to be present at the Royal Wedding.

Ghastly.

Horrendous.

Yet how differently the morning had started.

There was not the slightest hint of the vileness that was to follow.

There was joy and optimism in the air.

The sunlight glinted and sparkled on spider's web and dragonfly's wing.

Chiffchaffs sang. Swifts screeched.

Cocks crowed.

Cows lowed in the pastures below the massive earthwork of Botham's Gut.

The lady wife snored heavily in the conjugal container for all the world like a simmering tank locomotive at rest in some drowsy country branch-line siding.

I stepped carefully over the pink and twitching bellies of the slumbering Bedlington terriers.

Pausing only for a swift and successful foray on the bowel movement front, I padded softly downstairs and breakfasted alone on the terrace.

The spotted flycatcher flittered in the wistaria.

Swallows swooped low to scoop the dew from the lawn.

Through the open upstairs window I heard the creak of springs as the lady wife turned over in the bed of Procrustes, sounding for all the world like a rusty tramp steamer shifting at her moorings in some silted Flemish creek.

What bliss lay ahead.

A slow potter in the garden, an hour's brisk indoor pig-sticking with my neighbour, the commodore, and then snorters in his summer house, swapping cigarette cards, comparing train-spotters' notebooks and softly yawning the afternoon away – could a man ask for anything more perfect?

I sighed with deep contentment.

I scratched long and lingeringly all those dark and secret orifices forbidden to man by countless generations of lady wives and stern-chinned mamas.

I crept up behind the cat and shouted in its ear.

When the brute turned round, I flapped my arms and jumped up and down and it fled, ears flat on its head, into the gooseberry bushes.

It's the only way to treat them.

I sighed once more with satisfaction and began my inspection of the garden.

How beautiful it looked.

The clematis jackmanii was in full bloom, the fruits swelled proudly on the Coxon's orange pippins, the Eric Russell lupins stood out from the herbaceous alan border erect and rampant, the bernard hedges were clipped neat and tidy, the berries of the berberis don wilsonae sparkled and above all towered the noble stand of the cypress Maurice Leylandi.

My reveries were rudely interrupted by a stentorian

bellow from the french windows.

The lady wife!

Oh God, had I forgotten to flush the toilet again?

No.

She bellowed once more.

'It's already started. It's on the television.'

My heart missed a beat.

My blood froze in the veins.

Chill fingers of fear rilled down my spine.

Had I got it all wrong?

Had I made the most colossal boo-boo?

With a trembling voice, cracked with panic, I said:

'But I thought the Test match was next week.'

Instantly there appeared on the lady wife's brow dark and clustering furrows like the coal black isobars on a weather forecaster's chart, denoting impending storms in Portland Bill and Peter Wight, and imminent gales in Biscay and Fred Astaire.

'It's the Royal Wedding,' she hissed through those familiar threatening yellow equine teeth. 'And I want you inside. This instant.'

I am no coward, dear readers.

I have faced the bullets of Pathan, the sabres of Uhlan, the spears of fuzzy wuzzy, the poisoned darts of pygmy, the records of Barry Manilow and the cricket reports of Mr Tony Lewis, and I have not flinched.

But at that moment I knew the meaning of fear.

Real fear.

I knew how the novice jockey felt approaching Becher's Brook.

I knew how Keith Fletcher felt awaiting the umpire's decision at Delhi.

I knew how Rimsky felt the night before he married Korsakov.

And I gave in.

Abjectly I surrendered.

With bowed head and hunched shoulders I slunk across the lawn like Mr Ian Chappell returning to the pavilion after a heavily disputed clean-bowled decision had gone against him.

Cravenly I entered the drawing room and slumped into my armchair opposite the moving television screen.

I had to.

There was no other way.

I simply could not risk being 'gated' for the week of the Scarborough Festival.

There was nothing to do but watch the moving television screen and 'grin and bear it'.

Dear Lord above, what a palaver.

What a fuss.

Goodness knows how much the wallahs at the BBC spent on setting it up.

The procession alone must have cost them a small fortune.

Rank after rank of horses and on their backs rank after rank of silly asses wearing brass coal scuttles on their heads.

Open carriages jam-packed full of grinning, waving boobies with long necks and damp chins.

No wonder, we are having to pay more for our licences and sit through endless repeats of 'Terry and June'.

Sheer, wanton extravagance.

The money would have been better spent buying

decent shirts for the weather forecasters and investing in a new set of dentures for Mr Phil Drabble.

There was one moment of pleasure in the wretched business, I confess, when the bride alighted from her carriage outside the church.

How wonderful for our dear 'summer game', I felt, that one of the most loyal and honest of county cricketers, Mr Terry Spencer of Leicestershire, should have his daughter Diana thus elevated to the ranks of royalty.

Once inside the church, however, gloom descended again.

The porcine snufflings of the lady wife mingled with the frightful racket of the organ played, I suppose, as usual by Mr Robinson Cleaver, and the ghastly screechings of the bugles played by, what seemed to me, members of the band of Dr Crock and his Crackpots.

I looked around at the congregation.

Dear God, never in all my life had I seen such a collection of big ears.

And the faces!

Black faces, yellow faces, Muslim faces, Hindu faces, pock-marked faces, shifty faces, leering faces – it was like looking at a team photograph of Warwickshire County Cricket Club.

On and on and on droned the service.

Up and down bobbed the congregation like spectators behind the bowler's arm in the pavilion at the Oval.

Never have I felt such misery and despair.

And then?

And then of a sudden I felt my senses sharpening.

My muscles tensed. The adrenalin began to pump. The nerve ends tingled.

Something about the ceremony was 'not quite right'.

What was it?

What the devil was it?

Had they forgotten to invite Cliff Richard?

No.

There he was in the fifth row next to the Beverley Sisters and Mr Winston Place and wearing a natty green ostrich feather hat.

So what in the name of blitheration was it?

Realization dawned in a sudden blinding flash, when a creature purporting to be Mr George Thomas, Speaker of the House of Commons, rose to its feet to deliver the address.

Of course.

It wasn't George Thomas.

It was Mr Tony Lewis.

I could recognize those obsequious, snivelling, adenoidal Welsh cadences anywhere.

And what was he doing there?

No, it was not the usual reason – he was not auditioning for another crack at 'Grandstand'.

He was there for the same reason as everyone was there.

He was a stand-in.

It all fitted into place.

Because of the security problems, the authorities had trundled out a vast cast of extras to take the place of the genuine participants and guests.

Think back, dear readers.

Think back, I beg you.

Who was the Archbishop of Canterbury?

Think, think, think.

Of course, it was Mr E. W. 'Gloria' Swanton.

And who was Princess Margaret?

Dennis Lillee.

Without any effort at all I can reel off a list of dozens of stand-ins.

Princess Anne – David Gower.

Captain Mark Phillips – Keith Fletcher.

King Olav of Norway – Bill Alley.

Nancy Reagan – Dame Peter West.

Prince Charles – C. H. Dredge.

The King of Tonga – Fred Rumsey.

Page boy – Mr David Constant.

Her Majesty the Queen – Mr E. R. 'Elizabeth Regina' Dexter.

The Duke and Duchess of Kent, Mr Angus Ogilvie, the high commissioners for Canada, Australia and New Zealand, Garter King of Arms, Princess Alice of Athlone, the Queen of Denmark, Prince Edward, Prince Andrew, the ambassadors of Burma, Finland and Costa Rica, representatives of the Womens' Institute, the Girl Guides Association and the Post Office Advisory Committee – Mr Ian Botham.

And these suspicions were confirmed when some chap claiming to be Miss Kerria Chihuahua stood up and catawauled so loudly at the top of his voice that the confounded Bedlington terriers fled screaming to the utility room.

And who was it?

Of course, it was none other than Mr Joel Garner of Somerset and the West Indies, and he was wearing a silly frock.

The pleasure that suffused my whole being at this

discovery turned swiftly to euphoria.

It was not only the Royal Wedding which was all pretence.

So was the whole of life.

Consider Sir Geoffrey Howe, for example.

Think of that boring voice, those torpid eyes, the slow and sluggish clanking of the brain, the endless plodding of the intellect – he's the reincarnation of an innings by Trevor Bailey.

And who is playing the part of Willie Whitelaw?

Think, dear readers, think.

Of course – it's Frank Keating.

The list continues:

Sir Keith Joseph – Lance Gibbs.

Norman Tebbitt – Mr H. D. 'Dicky' Bird.

Dennis Healey – Clyde Walcott.

Rhodes Boyson – Sir Geoffrey Boycott.

Mrs Thatcher – Mr K. D. 'Slasher' MacKay of Queensland and Australia.

Michael Foot – Derek Randall.

Roy Hattersley, Cyril Smith, Andrew Faulds, Dame Judith Hart, Black Rod, Lord Hailsham, Edward du Cann, Edward du Cann't, Dafydd Wrigley-Spearmint, Dame Eric Heffer, Miss Gerald Kaufman, Mr Joan Lestor, the Rev Ian Parsley, the 1922 Committee, the Tribune Group, 'Diddy' Willie Hamilton, Mr Winsome Churchill, Doctor Gerard 'Frankie' Vaughn, Anthony Wedgwood-Benn, Tony Wedgwood, Anthony Benn, Tony Wedgwood-Benn, Big Ben, Miss Gwyneth Dogoody, Tony Benn, Ben Stansgate, Stan Bensgate, Sir Raymond Gower and his son, David, Tony Stansgate, Ben Wedgwood, Neil Pillock, the Serjeant at Arms,

William Pitt the Younger, Arthur Bottomley, Tony Wedgwood-Bottomley, Anthony Wedgwood-Benn the Younger, the Duke of Wellington, the Duke of Wedgwood, David Lloyd-George, Anthony Lloyd-Benn, Hitler, Mussolini, ex-King Zog, ex-King Ben, Dr Horace King, Lord Devlin and his daughter, Bernadette, Lord Denning and his son, Peter, God, and his son, Anthony Wedgwood-Benn – Mr Ian Botham.

I sat back in my armchair, cuffed the cat once more round the earholes, and it was as though I was surrounded by a shimmering and radiant glow.

Only I in the whole of the world knew the secret of life.

It was all pretence.

There is no reality.

All is impersonation.

All is . . .

And then I was struck by a cruel and sickening icy sword thrust into the innermost depths of my vitals.

If life is pretence, if there is no reality, then who the devil is impersonating the lady wife?

With mounting horror and panic I looked at her.

Dear God, what I had long suspected was true.

For the past fifty years I had been having 'relations' with Mr Denis Compton.

20
Hard Times

Dear readers, these are indeed hard times for lovers of our dear 'summer game'.

There is no doubt that it is now facing the severest and profoundest threat it has ever been called upon to meet in its entire glorious and noble history.

It is quite literally having to fight for survival.

Consider some of the facts:

The world's reserves of pad whitener and stumpers' gloves are rapidly dwindling to the point of no return.

A series of seven calamitous summers have devastated the world crop of sweat bands and floppy-brimmed sun hats.

And, if the Arabs place any more restrictions on the

supply of linseed oil, God knows what the lady wife's loathsome spinster sister will use for soaking her dentures overnight.

We face, too, these days a crucial and frightening shortage of cricket 'craftsmen'.

There remain in this country today only two makers of musical jockstraps, and these are both well into their eighties and rapidly approaching infirmity and terminal drunkenness.

The Japanese have 'cornered the market' in bat mallets and abdominal protectors, and German success in the field of thigh pads and netting poles has completely destroyed a once thriving export industry in Keating New Town.

How sickening to see thousands of young men, the cream of our manhood, the joyous fruits of our loins, going out to bat dressed in Volkswagen disposable underpants and Toyota digital arch supports.

And what of the values long cherished by all devotees of our blessed 'summer game'?

In ruins.

In tatters.

Day by day the old virtues of fair play and sportsmanship, of manly courage and gracious chivalry are being massacred by boot-toting Australian fast bowlers, cheque book-waving entrepreneurs with inside-out faces and illicit midnight feasts with tuck boxes and 'fast' umpires in the radio commentary box at Trent Bridge.

How Dame Peter West must long for a return to his sequins and his surgical dancing pumps.

At times like this, dear readers, there are but two

comforts to console men of a cricketing bent – the church and the bottle.

Let us, therefore, crack open a bottle of our favourite Voce and Larwood finest dry Madeira, light up a pipeful of Captain Lock's rum-flavoured shag and seek the solace of the church.

Through what means shall we achieve this?

Simple.

Through the agency of the works of the Rev. A. K. Mole-Drably.

Readers of a previous book written by that verminous lout, Tinniswood, may recall a sermon I recounted, which had been given by Mole-Drably at the service designated in the Book of Common Prayer as 'the Third Sunday after the Lords Test'.

The text of that sermon was thus:

'And, behold, Ron Saggers did tour England with the 1948 Australians and, lo, not a single Test match did he play in.'

Many of you were kind enough to communicate with me by unstamped letter or reverse charge phone call to apprise me of the comfort this sermon had brought you.

'Bedwetter' of Basingstoke wrote as follows:

'I have these strange urges when I want to take off all my clothes during the second day of the Edgbaston Test and rub my body with dubbin and cloves cordial. Have you, by any chance, a signed photo of Mr Don Mosey in the nude?'

And from Castle Arlott a lady wrote:

'I cannot tell you how much I identified with Ron Saggers. In the past I had always felt a certain sympathy for the other 'Ron'. I refer, of course to Mr Ron

Hamence of South Australia. An illustrated booklet of the Australian Tour to England, 1948, in my possession describes Mr Hamence thus: 'Once set he is a very difficult man to shift.' How like my dear departed husband, the mobile librarian. However, on reading the Rev. Mole-Drably's inspiring sermon I repaired immediately to the aforesaid booklet and there read the following words relating to Mr Saggers: 'Given an opportunity is sure to please.' My late second husband, the piano tuner, was given the opportunity many many times and never once failed to please. Do you by any chance know the marital status of Mr Graham Roope and have you a signed picture of Mr Trevor Bailey in frogman's suit and lacrosse boots? Isn't cricket sexy?'

I confess that I have never looked on our dear 'summer game' in that light, although there have been occasions when watching the run up to the wicket of the immortal Mr D. V. P. Wright of Kent and England that I have experienced vague feelings of restlessness in the nether regions of the popping crease.

However, back to the Rev. Mole-Drably and the comfort to be gained from his sacerdotal ministrations.

You may recall that on the last occasion we encountered him he was the holder of the rectorship of the church of St Wilfred the Blessed Rhodes, in the county of Yorkshire.

No longer, I fear, no longer.

Poor soul, he it was who was the principal victim of what is now known to historians of the 'summer game' as the Yorkshire Schism of '81.

It is not for me to pass comment on the Jesuitical

casuistries and Mafia-like intrigues of the general synod of Yorkshire CCC.

These are far too complex and complicated for laymen to cope with and are only to be completely understood in the innermost recesses of the Vatican and the most sacred ministries of the *Daily Telegraph* sports department.

Suffice it to say that after the banishment of St John Hampshire to Derbyshire, Mole-Drably found himself in the impossible position of having to choose between the theory of divine omnipotence as proposed by St Raymond D'Illingworth or the 'Fitzwilliam Heresy' of Bishop Boycott.

Our friend chose to side with the latter, and thus found himself instantly deprived of his living with the swiftness of a Chris Old declaring himself unfit to play in a West Indies Test Match.

Times were indeed hard for him thereafter.

An unhappy period acting as baggage master and scorer for Mr Gerald Priestland was followed by a spell as part-time padre to the Wombwell Cricket Lovers' Society and personal confessor to Mr Cliff Richard.

At length, like most of the pathetically few Yorkshire heretics who have escaped being burned at the stake at Bramall Lane, flogged, hung, drawn and quartered at Bradford, stoned at Leeds and tarred and feathered at Scarborough (in that order of play), he sought sanctuary in the bleak and near inaccessible monasteries of the Derbyshire Orthodox Church.

That beloved, chaste and virtuous leader of the Church, His Blissful and Sublime Holiness the Archpatriarch Barry Wood, clasped him warmly in his arms, kissed him thrice upon the cheeks and uttered in his silken, melliflous voice those ancient and moving words of welcome laid down by the prophets of his church so many centuries earlier:

'Hey up, shite face. All right?'

He was conducted by Brother Steele and Brother Taylor to a sparse but comfortable cell in the monastery of St Fred de Swarbrook high in the peaks above Tideswell.

As he dined off Rhodes in the hole, fricasee of wild Dawkes and Revilled kidneys washed down by liberal draughts of Harvey-Walkerbangers, the kindly old abbot and scholar, Father Cliffordus Gladwinius, read aloud to him from the works of Chaucer.

For Mole-Drably it was as though a great weight had been lifted from his mind as he listened to the abbot reciting those well-loved tales that have so charmed and comforted cricketers over the ages:

'Roger Knight's Tale.'

'Keith Miller's Tale.'

'Charlie Cook's Tale.'

'Vijay Merchant's Tale.'

And, of course:

'The Wife of Botham's Tale.'

For the first time in many months he slept soundly and as he awoke to the dawn chorus of peewit and pipit and the chanted devotions of aged medium-pacers, he resolved there and then that he would dedicate the whole of the rest of his life to the writing of sacred books.

I have in my possession now some of these works, and

they occupy a place of pride and prominence in my study at Witney Scrotum.

It is from one of these works, *A Treasury of Sermons for Distressed Cricketfolk*, that I present to you this most soothing of pieces:

A Sermon for Stumpers Stricken by Piles.

'And, lo, it is written in *Wisden* of 1981, page 202 under the heading "Four Wickets with Consecutive Balls" the following words:

'"S. N. Mohol . . . Board of Control President's XI versus Minister for Small Savings XI, Poona."

'I find great comfort in those words.

'You see, they mean, don't they, that however large a saver we are in the bank of life, or however small a saver we are, there is always the chance of being selected to play for God's XI.

'It might not be against the Board of Control President's XI at Poona.

'It could indeed be against Northants Seconds at Corby.

'But whatever the match at whatever the venue we know, don't we, that we will be awarded our "cap".

'As far as God is concerned, we are all in the running for representative honours – particularly if we can "do a bit" with the new ball.

'You see, wherever we may be, in Poona or in Perth, in Swansea or in Srinagar, in Brisbane or in Bath, we are being watched by the Infinite Being from his stool in the eternal long room bar.

'Whatever we may do, a "blob" at Sabina Park, a "hit wicket" at Amritsar, a decision to "dispense with bails" at Bangalore, an unprovoked attack of the Nawab of Pataudis at Madras, our actions are being noted in the books of the Immortal Twelve Apostles, chairman the Marchioness, Peter May.

'In whatever league we may "wield the willow" or caress "the crimson rambler", in Sheffield Shield or Currie Cup, in Ranji Trophy or Cornhill Test, we can be sure the Celestial Correspondent will send his report to *Wisden* and the *Daily Telegraph* and the word will prevail, and woe be to him who disputes that word.

'Who, you may ask, is S. N. Mohol?

'Who was stumper for Board of Control President's XI?

'Who was the Minister for Small Savings and did he give the four victims of S. N. Mohol a thorough good bollocking?

'Poor sinners all, we have no idea, have we?

'Our comfort must lie in the knowledge that when that great Umpire in the sky removes our bails at "stumps" and we are summoned to the great timeless Test of Immortality, all shall be revealed.

'I am often asked: Is there cricket after death?

'Yes.

'Oh yes.

'That I believe fervently, passionately, with a blinding faith as strong as the faith which maintains that the mouth of Mr Ritchie Benaud bears a remarkable resemblance to a hamster's arsehole.

'There *is* cricket after death.

'In this we must believe.

'How else to explain the price of beer at Old Trafford and the state of the pork pies at Lords?

'How else to explain an innings by Mr Trevor Bailey?

'How else to explain the cricket reports of Mr Tony Lewis?

'There must be something more to life than that?

'Of course there is.

'There is death.

'And these are but the trials and tribulations we must all bear to prepare ourselves for the better life to come, when all earthly cares are lifted from our worthless bodies and our souls ascend to Heaven in a soaring, joyous upward curve like a mighty six from the noble blade of Mr Ian Botham.

'And when the heavenly senior citizen gatekeeper lets us through the turnstiles of the pearly gates, and we affix our eternal "wanderers" ticket to our purest silk John Edrich autograph shrouds, we shall find Paradise.

'And what is the Paradise, to which we all aspire?

'A cricket ground basked in autumnal sum.

'Shimmering oaks and copper beeches.

'Swallows skimming, bees droning and those noble words ringing high into the limpid air:

'"Will the owner of car FAA 811W kindly report to the secretary's tent. He's causing an obstruction outside the Taverner's Fruit-drop shop."

'And we shall recline in our deck chair, and we shall draw a mug of foaming ale to our lips and there before us in the eternal glow of our Timeless Test we shall see our heroes play.

'Jack Hobbs and W. G., Herbert Sutcliffe and Victor Trumper, E. A. McDonald and 'Tich' Freeman, J. B. Statham and Roy Tattersall, W. B. Roberts and Bob Berry, J. T. Ikin and Alan Wharton, Willie Watson and

J. G. Binks, E. H. Edrich and the blessed Winston Place.

'And we shall preen ourselves with pleasure, and the juices will flow sweet and languid in our veins, and, cricket being cricket, it will start to piss down and we'll get soaked right down to our vests.

'But let us not worry.

'That great Groundsman in the sky has secured his covers.

'There will be no leakages.

'And when the sun appears again, as appear it always will, there will be no "sticky dog" and play will be resumed on time.

'All will be peace and serenity as the Timeless Test progresses.

'There will be no lady streakers with things on their chests.

'The voice of John Arlott will be heard in the land once more.

'Beer will not be dispensed in plastic beakers.

'There will be no advertisements on the boundary fence for Pakistan Airlines or Toyota tractors.

'And when at close of play, we return to our homes, there will be no lady wives to rap our wrists as we attempt to change channels from "Hawai Five O" to "Test Match Special".

'And when we repair to our beds, we shall dream sweet dreams.

'Bowling out Don Bradman first ball.

'Thrashing Fred Trueman through the covers for four after four after four.

'Catching Vivian Richards for a duck on the far long on boundary.

'Being allowed to carry Ian Botham's cricket bag.

'Yes, yes, there is cricket after death.

'And those of you who dedicate your lives to God will play it eternally on those celestial pastures when your innings on earth is declared closed.

'For those of you who don't, it's everlasting rugby league.

'My next sermon will take as its text:

'"And, lo, Harry Halliday was a plump man, yet many a six did he smite for Yorkshire."'

I take great solace from these words, dear readers, don't you?

21
The Mole

I shall not prevaricate.

I know the name of the Mole in the MCC.

I am certain beyond the slightest shadow of doubt that I can reveal the identity of the person who 'tipped off' Burgess of Somerset, MacLean of South Africa and Alan 'Kim' Phebey of Kent.

His name is . . .

But wait.

Is it not better (to use the immortal words of Mr E. R. 'Elizabeth Regina' Dexter) 'to let sleeping dogs lie'?

The damage has already been done.

What possible good can come from the re-opening of old wounds?

And yet. . .

Yet when I think of the baseness of his behaviour, the vileness of his treachery and the voraciousness of his cupidity, my blood boils, my temples throb and the visor of my MCC sun cap hisses with steam.

Consider, dear readers, just a few of the evils perpetrated by this 'creature'.

For forty years, while occupying a position of deep trust with some of 'the highest in the land' he was actually selling to the Kremlin top secret, highly classified documents recording every single decision made by the English selectors over four decades.

What 'gold' for the Russian scum.

Just think of the implications.

The Russians actually knew before Mr E. W. 'Gloria' Swanton why Cliff Gladwin was dropped for the Fourth Test match against South Africa in 1947 and replaced by Harold Butler of Nottingham.

And it is certain that with the connivance of the Mole and KGB agents it was Russian influence which secured for Butler, when he retired from first class cricket, the position of Chancellor of the Exchequer, which, of course, to use more of Mr E. R. 'Elizabeth Regina' Dexter's noble prose, 'explains a lot'.

Worse is to follow.

With infiltration of this sort in operation can we be certain that the Russians were not, in fact, manipulating the decisions of the English selectors?

If this theory is accepted, it accounts for many of the inexplicable actions of the 'inner cabinet' which have occupied the minds of some of the world's greatest historians over the past century.

Why, for example, did Mr Tommy Greenhough play only four times for England?

Why was the great and saintly Winston Place never selected to play against Australia?

Why was Mr Alan Wharton not called upon to bowl in either of New Zealand's innings in the First Test match at Headingley in 1949, dropped for the next Test and subsequently never chosen to play for his country again?

A solution to this last question has baffled minds as great as that of the magnificent Mr J. M. 'Aubrey' Brearley.

But now we have the answer.

And it's a simple one – Russian agents were at work in the innermost vitals of the cricketing establishment.

And they were there through the efforts of one man and one man alone, whose name is. . .

No.

He is an old man.

He lives in peaceful retirement in the heart of our beautiful English countryside surrounded by his dogs and his books and cared for with love and affection by his two ex-Royal Navy 'spinster' friends.

Is it fair to them to rake through the ashes?

And yet. . .

Yet when I think of the enormity of his duplicity during the Second World War, I am consumed by a rage so violent it can only be assuaged by the swift application of my boot end to the rib cages of the lady wife's confounded Bedlington terriers.

Forget that loathsome bounder, Blunt, and his wife, Lyn Fontaine.

His treachery was a pale milk sop compared with that perpetrated by the Mole in the dark days of the last year of the war when the pavilion of our beloved Bramall Lane was used as a barrage balloon hangar, an adaptation which was to help Mr Fred Rumsey many years later while changing his underpants.

I can scarcely bring myself to describe the actions of the Mole.

But I must.

I owe it to my country.

So, gritting my teeth, flexing my upper lip and easing the elastic of my abdominal protector, I have to tell you, dear readers, that . . .

No.

Before I do, I must insist that you are seated, are of sound blood pressure and have within easy reach an extensive stock of strong drink.

These conditions are vital for your health and well-being, such is the enormity of the calumny I am now about to reveal.

Are you ready?

Here goes:

In the spring of 1944 the Mole actually passed on to agents of the German High Command in Berlin the blueprints of Gunn and Moore's new Charlie Barnett autograph cricket bat.

There.

The secret is out, and I feel relieved, for it has been a heavy burden to have borne alone for so long.

But is this the 'end of the affair'?

Can I in all conscience leave it at that?

Do I not have a bounden obligation to the land of my

birth and the members of the *Sunday Times* Insight team to reveal the traitor's name?

I feel I have.

So here goes. His name is. . .

No.

He is a sick man.

Publicity of this sort could kill him, of that I have not the slightest doubt.

Let us, therefore, draw a veil over the whole affair.

Let us content ourselves with revealing only the sketchiest and vaguest of details concerning the identity of this poor, misbegotten, misguided creature.

He was born at 4.37 a.m. on the morning of June 18th, 1903, in the small Lancashire village of Cardus-in-Tyldesleydale, which lies some five miles due east of the Trough of Bolus.

He attended the village school of St Cecil de Parkin, of which his father was headmaster and his mother chief groundsman and boilerman.

His academic prowess won him an open scholarship to Manchester Grammar School, which he attended from the years 1914 to 1921, when he 'went up' to Cambridge University to read political philosophy, classical Persian, difficult sums and the history of Derbyshire County Cricket Club, 1896 to 1919.

It was there that I first met him.

Now as I sit in my study at Witney Scrotum and see in the garden a flock of goldcrests and long-tailed tits quartering the conifers, a pair of bullfinches sullenly brooding in the apple tree and the lady wife perched high on the roof of the commodore's summer house, her blow lamp flaring, as she resolders the spurs back on to the weather cock, I think back to those distant and blissful days of honeyed youth.

It was indeed the 'golden age'.

Everything a civilized man could desire for the 'full life' flourished and prospered.

Draughty trams still rattled the narrow streets of cobbled Pennine towns, sailing barges still plied the muddied Broadland creeks, steam locomotives huffed and puffed up Lickey Bank, Cunarders fretted the waves at Mersey Bar, the blessed red rose of Lancashire was red and rampant.

It was the age of the sublime Harry Makepeace, the immaculate Ernest Tyldesley and the immortal E. A. McDonald and his opening bowling partner, Miss Nelson Eddy.

It was the age of O. S. Nock and the inimitable Robertson Glasgow and his dearly loved catch phrase; 'Oh, Calamity'.

There was not the slightest hint of impending Cliff Richards or Petunia Clark.

Life was gracious and elegant, and high society was bewitched and entranced by the beauty and wit of Lady Henry Cooper and Dame Peter West.

It was in this atmosphere of peace and serenity that I first met the Mole.

He was a 'correct' young man.

His togs were 'decent'.

His manner was diffident but friendly.

He had a firm handshake.

Dear God, I had no idea he was a bugger, a sodomite and a nancy boy to boot.

I confess I had my doubts about his chum, Nigel,

whose flowered shirt and crushed greengage-coloured velvet pantaloons made me suspect that he was not, as the Mole averred, the opening bowling partner of Mr Reg Perks of Worcestershire and England.

I felt, too, that Aubrey and Hector, despite the Mole's earnest protestations, were not members of the Leicestershire CCC ground staff with special responsibility for the maintenance of Mr L. G. Berry's toenails.

I suppose in those days I was an innocent.

I had not 'cottoned on'.

I sincerely believed that life was inherently nice, that the sun would never set on the British Empire, that the 'fairer sex' and all amateur county cricket players were totally lacking in pubic hair.

Imagine my shock on my first sight of Mr Kenneth Cranston 'in the buff'.

Imagine my mortification, too, on discovering that the Mole was (to use the delicate and sensitive prose of Mr E. R. 'Elizabeth Regina' Dexter) a 'raging poofta and a screaming bender'.

How could I have suspected it?

My friend's credentials were impeccable.

After coming down from Cambridge he passed his entrance examinations to MCC with 'flying colours'.

Within the year he was appointed chief of chancery of the MCC mission to the Vatican, where he became chief instructor in leg breaks and googlies to the Holy Father.

After only six months in that post he was elevated to the position of Chief Administrator (Cricket) MCC Antarctic Territories, where he was instrumental in developing the blubber-powered heavy roller for use in Old Trafford Test matches.

Thereafter his promotion was swift and spectacular:

1926–1931 *chef de cabinet* to Mr E. W. 'Gloria' Swanton at the *Daily Telegraph*.

1931–1933 League of Nations permanent delegate to Yorkshire County Cricket Club.

1933–1937 MCC ambassador to the court of King Zog of Albania where he introduced the printed score card and the tea interval.

1937–1939 private tutor to Mr H. D. 'Dicky' Bird.

It was then he achieved the ultimate accolade of being appointed to the MCC Museum at Lords as chief curator, jock straps.

We now know, however, that that was but 'a front'.

The Mole's real job was head of counter intelligence in MCC, the so-called, Cambridge-dominated Dewesieme Bureau.

It was the pinnacle of his career of treachery.

It was what his Russian masters had worked for all those years since they had suborned him in Cambridge by taking photographs of him of a compromising nature involving a cardboard cut-out model of Mr Leslie Saroney, a pair of Mr 'Patsy' Hendren's underpants and an inflatable rubber sightscreen.

He was a puppet to the strings pulled by the KGB.

Does that excuse his traitorous activities?

Who am I to say?

I am not God or Robin Marlar.

Certainly in all those years I knew him I had not the slightest reason to suspect the double role he was playing.

How was I to know that throughout the whole of the Second World War and the subsequent confrontations of the cold war he was supplying information to Russian and German alike?

When I visited him during the last war he always seemed such a normal chap as he sat in the madeira lace hammock on his lawn, idly tossing greengage pips at the doodlebugs chugging overhead and smiling with benign pleasure as he watched the tattoos rippling on the forearms of his two ex-Royal Navy 'spinster' friends as they knitted trench comforters in pink angora for the lads from the nearby ack ack battery.

The hock he served on those occasions was always exquisite and never once did I have cause to complain about the quality of his caviar.

And yet all the time the loathsome stinker was passing secrets to his masters in Moscow and Berlin.

What were those secrets?

I cannot be certain.

I am not God or Barry Took.

I am, however, convinced that it was he who passed on to the Russians the top-secret information that MCC would indeed open an Eastern Front by allowing Essex CCC to play first-class county cricket at Southend.

He it was, too, who was consistently passing highly-classified information to the Russians during the Great Powers crisis of 1950/51 which reached its culmination with the airlift of Tattersall to Australia.

Call me naive, if you will, but I suspected nothing when he quizzed me for information regarding the combination of the lock on Mr E. W. 'Gloria' Swanton's *Roget's Thesaurus*.

I took it as quite natural that he should show a keen interest in the latest opening batting experiments conducted on the test beds at Lords by Mr Sam 'Werner Von' Brown.

And I confess I found nothing to alarm me when he asked:

'If Hitler were to conquer and occupy England, do you think Yorkshire would allow Germans to play for their county?'

I said I was convinced they would, as their committee seemed to consist entirely at that time of members of the Gestapo and close relatives of Hermann Goering.

Yes, I was a blind fool, I admit.

Even so, dear readers, charity and hindsight compel me to confess that in my heart of hearts I am prepared to forgive him for these treacheries.

And for what reason?

Because, dear readers, he claims that he did not as the *Sunday Times* and Mr Chapman Snitcher would have us believe give away secrets to this country's bitterest and most unforgiving of enemies (I refer, of course, to Australia) but was, in fact, working all the time as a 'double agent'.

I have no means of confirming this.

I have no means of disproving it.

I am not God or Roy Plomley.

All I can do is present for your judgment the 'facts' he presented to me on the last occasion I visited him.

He claims that it was he who before the crucial final Test match at the Oval in 1953 passed on to the Australian skipper, Mr Lindsay Hassett, the information – incorrect as we now know – that Mr G. A. R. Lock had secretly become a deacon of the Church of Fullers the Avenger, and would thus refuse to bowl in

Australia's second innings on religious grounds – or indeed any other grounds for that matter.

Did this false information completely alter the tactics of the minute, large-eared Australian skipper and so hand the match to England 'on a plate'?

Who can say?

I most certainly cannot, for I am not God or Clive James.

Incidentally, according to the Mole, Clive James is not all he is 'cracked up' to be.

He is, in fact, the reincarnation of Archie Andrews, although my friend steadfastly refuses to reveal who is working him.

I will not detain you with intricate details of his other revelations.

Suffice it for me to answer a few of the burning questions which these disclosures will raise in your minds.

Yes, it *was* Edgar Britt's riding boots.

No, Mr Keith Miller did not say that to Miss Iris Murdoch, although he might have said it to Edgar Britt.

No, Jan Morris is not the sister of Mr A. R. Morris.

Seven times, if we include the half-hour session in the curator's portable commode at Perth.

Dame Vera Lynn, Max Walker, Jean Rhys, Ian Chappell, Miss Margaret Drabble and her father, Phil, Keith Miller and Mr H. D. 'Dicky' Bird.

The *salon privé* at Edgbaston, July 12th, 1968.

Flatulence.

His wife would not allow him.

Seven and a half inches.

In Mr David Constant's panama hat.

How do I know? I am not God or O. S. Nock, although, by jingo, I wish I were the latter.

One vital question remains to be answered.

How did the Mole pass on this information to his masters?

By clandestine meetings in midnight gents urinals, by hollows in lonely wayside trees, by homing pigeon, by high-powered radio?

No.

It is simpler than that.

The information was passed through coded messages in *Wisden's Cricketers' Almanack*.

Yes, take another long draught of your strong liquor, dear readers, for it is indeed a terrible and most grievous shock I know.

But we must steel ourselves and face the truth with fortitude – our "bible" has been irretrievably dispoiled.

Who can ever read its noble prose again without a cringe of outrage, a sickening of the soul, a silent howl of despair?

And where does the key to the code lie?

In a simple passage in the *Almanack* of 1948 contained in the first paragraph of page 642.

I quote:

Abundant sunshine brought fresh vigour and zest into Scottish cricket in 1947, more interest than ever being taken in the game. Many English visitors seemed surprised to find cricket quite so well played and intelligently followed, and, on being told that as many as ten thousand people would watch a local 'Derby' such as Perthshire versus Forfarshire, their surprise was increased still further.

Dear God, it is too much to bear.

I will, I will, I will.

I will reveal the dastardly traitor's name.

It is. . .

No.

Let us give him a taste of his 'own medicine'.

You have the code, dear readers.

Work it out for yourselves.

His name is contained in this passage from page 942 of *Wisden's Almanack*, 1950:

A player or umpire will be paid the cost of a first class railway fare from the ground on which he was last engaged or from his home if he has not been immediately engaged prior to the Test Match. He will similarly be paid the cost of a first class railway fare to the ground on which he is next engaged or to his home if he is not so engaged. If a player or umpire travels by car he may claim the equivalent railway fare as stipulated above, but may not claim garage charges in addition.

No, God damn it, it is *not* Nancy Banks-Smith.

Try again.

22
Apartheid

Like all lovers of the 'summer game' I am appalled at the beastliness surrounding MCC's recent tour to India.

To quote the memorable and stunningly majestic words of tne distinguished journalist, essayist, poet, philosopher and biographer of Mr Michael Parkinson, Mr E. R. 'Elizabeth Regina' Dexter:

'It's a rum old world we live in.'

I agree.

Indeed I am tempted to be even more provocative and at the risk of courting widespread public odium and being refused service in the village dog biscuit shop, state quite categorically and without reservation of any sort that I am all in favour of apartheid.

Before condemning me out of hand, dear readers, I beg of you to search deep into your hearts and your consciences.

Go on.

Admit it.

You know it's true.

They are not like us.

Scientists have proved conclusively that they are inferior beings in every respect.

They are inferior mentally.

They are inferior emotionally.

And while they may be stronger physically, their moral fibre is most certainly of the flimsiest nature.

Let us not beat about the bush – we find their appearance revolting, don't we?

And we know that their presence in civilized western society is totally disruptive and the cause of most of the major disasters that have afflicted us this century.

So why on earth do they want to live in our midst?

It is a proven fact of nature that basically and deep down they are at their happiest and their most harmless when they are 'amongst their own'.

So why should they be allowed to travel in the same trains as us, to drink at the same clubs, to live in the same neighbourhoods, and, horror of horror, be admitted to that bastion of all that is most noble and honourable and precious in this dear country of ours – the cricket pavilion?

Good God, they are women.

And we are men.

And, as far as I am concerned, 'ne'er the twain shall meet'.

The more observant amongst you, dear readers, will probably have noticed that there are certain differences of a physical nature between us.

'They' have certain appendages which we just do not have.

In this context I refer specifically to loud voices, hairy legs and sharp shins.

'They' have also what I can only describe as 'things' on the front of their chests, which play havoc with the shape of long-cherished cricket sweaters, which they insist on wearing when taking their confounded Bedlington terriers ratting in the coppice at Cowdrey's Bottom or mucking out the stables at their loathsome unmarried sister's establishment at . . .

No.

I must restrain myself.

With all the calmness and sweet reason I can muster I place my case before you simply and without embellishment of any sort – we are two totally separate races and it is against the law of nature that we should mix.

Look around, dear readers.

Consider all the happy and contented bachelors you know.

The Bedser twins, for example.

Can one possibly imagine the carnage and mayhem that would ensue if a bold, wild woman aflood with the reckless passion and the hot-blooded Latin sensuousness of a Keith Fletcher were to get her hands on them?

Disaster.

In an instant she would rip from their backs their immaculate, hand-tailored Subba Row grey worsted suits.

In a frenzy she would wrench from their feet their immaculate, hand-tailored British Home Stores black nylon socks.

And what would she place in their stead?

There is not the slightest shadow of a doubt that she would choose for the poor, gibbering wretches crushed-gooseberry PVC catsuits and purple velvet moon boots.

Now this type of togs is suitable enough for sartorial rebels like Mr E. W. 'Gloria' Swanton or Mr Donald Carr and his sister, Pearl, or Captain Mark Phillipson, son of the former distinguished Lancashire cricketer and umpire, Eddie.

But for the Bedser twins?

No.

Not at all.

They have no need of vestmental adornment to 'bring out' their natural gazelle-like gracefulness of form.

Like the pavilion at Lords, the outside toilets at the Garrick Club and the cardinals' sun lounge and sauna at the Vatican they should be kept completely free of women.

Consider their mischievous humour, their constant, bounding high spirits, their ever-sparkling eyes, the spring and lilt to their step, the twinkling animation of their voices – they are living proof that man without woman is a creature of nobility and towering strength.

When I think of women and the role they play in contemporary society (bus drivers, professional racing cyclists, members of Parliament of both sexes) I confess 'they've got me stumped'.

At the risk of appearing irreverent I have to state that I simply cannot understand what the Almighty was thinking of when he made them different from men.

I accept without reservation that it has been the making of ladies' netball.

But at what cost, I ask myself.

Consider the multifarious horrors this one act of divine madness has inflicted on us – mixed ballroom dancing, long fingernails, the ink monitor at Number Ten, knitting patterns, arguments, overlarge handbags, vile continental holidays during the week of the Scarborough Festival, confounded Bedlington terriers with pink bellies and fleas, loathsome spinster sisters incessantly sucking mint imperials.

I am aware that there are poor, misguided souls who maintain that women were created for the sole purpose of the propagation of the species.

Well, like all lovers of our dear 'summer game' I believe that that particular activity is a grossly overrated pastime.

There is far too much grunting and sharp toenails involved.

There are some so-called experts with their dandruff and ill-knitted Fair Isle pullovers who take great pains to inform us that the average man gets more exercise out of 'doing it' than he would out of playing a full match of rugby union football.

That may well be the case.

But I maintain that rugby union football is a damn sight more exciting and there are infinitely more tactics involved.

I am forced to the conclusion that the 'fly in the ointment' as regards the propagation of the species is the human reproduction system.

How much more satisfactory it would be if the lady wife were to lay an egg and sit on it for nine months until the wretched thing hatched out.

Dear readers, just think of all the advantages.

The lady wife would be confined to the house for nine solid months seated on her egg reading back numbers of *Pins and Needles*.

What possible excuse could she then have for accompanying you to the village pub at Witney Scrotum?

Ah yes, I know what she'd say.

'I could always stick the egg in the oven for a while,' she'd say in those familiar odious hectoring tones.

Absolute balderdash and tommyrot.

How could one rely on it with the state of the gas pressure these days?

It is patently obvious what would happen.

The oven would be switched on at regulo two. The egg would be placed inside. The man and his lady wife would stroll down to the village hostelry for two brief 'snorters' and a half an hour's nagging about the state of his underpants, and, when they returned home, the gas pressure would have gone up and they would discover that their son and heir has been turned into a Spanish omelette.

It just is not on.

I have explained the situation umpteen times to the lady wife, but still she insists on the statutory hanky-panky even at the height of winter during a commentary of England versus West Indies at Port of Spain.

Dear God, no wonder Bob Willis was no-balled seventeen times.

The whole trouble with women is that they will insist

on poking their long, over-powdered noses into affairs which by their very physical nature they simply cannot understand.

Take MCC tours to foreign parts, for example.

I am convinced that society as we know it in its pre-Petunia Clark heyday of Thermogene, Gillie Potter and wet battery wirelesses started to 'go to the dogs' as soon as the authorities allowed players' wives to accompany them on overseas tours.

How can 'our lads' concentrate on the matter in hand when they are being constantly harangued about the price of sprouts, the iniquitous behaviour of Nelson Gabriel in 'The Archers', the state of disorder of their sponge bags and the welfare of the confounded Bedlington terriers in their kennels at Langridge-on-Sea.

I don't give a damn about the welfare of the Bedlington terriers.

What possible concern of mine can it be that the lady wife has once again forgotten to cancel the papers?

Is it my fault that her loathsome spinster sister is unable to work the time clock on her central heating and. . .

No.

I must restrain myself.

I am a reasonable man, and I state publicly without prevarication that the institution of marriage has a great deal to recommend it.

It is only the presence of women in it which makes it so damnable.

I am prepared to 'go on record' and tell you, dear readers, that if it were not the custom for a man to marry a woman, I should without a moment's hesitation have plighted my troth to Mr Fred Rumsey.

Good God, at least he would have kept me warm in bed, and there is no doubt that his cooking would have been vastly superior to that of the lady wife.

Even now I shudder to the very core of my soul when I consider her culinary activities.

In the early days of our marriage I used to wait until she had left the room to fix the overflow of the lavatory, and then I would give the food she had prepared to our late-lamented Lancashire setter, Pollard.

Poor devil, it simply could not stand it.

One day it ran away, and it was three weeks before it was discovered attempting to tunnel its way into the free-range hamster farm at Keating New Town.

When I went round to the station pound to collect it, the poor brute threw back its head and howled.

It wagged its tail, it jumped up at my shoulders, and it looked at me with those great liquid brown pleading eyes.

I simply hadn't the heart to bring it home.

No, the whole problem with modern society is that marriage is being submerged by the vast amount of advice doled out by so-called experts.

What a ghastly shower.

What on earth was that pious and virginal Surrey and England batsman and slip fielder, Mr Grahame Roope, thinking of to allow his mother, Marjorie, to churn out such abominable claptrap each week in the *Daily Mirror* newspaper?

The much-respected New Zealand Test cricketer, Mr Geoffrey Rabone, has a great deal to answer for inflicting on us his odious mother, Anna.

And who could have imagined that that great polar explorer, Nansen, would one day torment us with his revolting, self-opinionated daughter, Esther?

The plain fact of the matter is that there is only one piece of advice which needs to be given to the younger generation when they are considering marriage.

It is this:

Never marry a beautiful woman.

If a man is foolhardy enough to marry a beautiful woman with a sweet disposition, his life is made an utter misery.

You see, dear readers, it is axiomatic that 'nice' people have always got more relations than people like us.

And what function do relations perform in the absurd hurly burly of life?

They place your home in a state of constant siege, borrowing the colander, frightening the budgerigar, using excessive amounts of toilet paper and showing interminable series of snapshots of their disgusting offspring winning fancydress competitions on P&O liners.

It is beyond dispute that the marital home should be a haven of despair and desolation, an oasis of rampant inhospitality. And, my friends, it is only a very ugly woman with a very ugly temper who will provide those conditions.

That is the only consolation I draw from the constant presence in my home of the lady wife.

In the early days of our married life her ugliness was such that on one occasion a close friend of mine, the curator of the golf ball museum in Witney Scrotum, was prompted to ask:

'Excuse me, but do you ever have "relations" with your wife?'

I answered:

'Yes.'

He responded:

'Why?'

'Simple,' I replied. 'I want to see what it is like "doing it" with a very ugly woman.'

'And what is it like "doing it" with a very ugly woman?' he asked.

'The same as "doing it" with a very beautiful woman, I imagine,' I replied. 'Slightly better than toothache. Not a patch on the Saturday of the Lords Test.'

I fear, however, that these observations of mine will fall on the deaf ears of the younger generation.

Poor fools, they are 'carried away' by the so-called romance and glamour of marriage – nights of passion in the boudoir, transparent negligees, dollops of talcum powder flung into the bottom of MCC bedsocks.

But in all this euphoria they ignore one crucial and fundamental fact about marriage as we know it – it involves sleeping with a woman.

And that is the ultimate punishment known to man.

What people simply do not realize is that as soon as a woman falls asleep she automatically doubles her body weight.

She closes her eyes, she begins to twitch and snore, she keels over on to you and – wop – it is like sleeping under the heavy roller at Trent Bridge.

Mind you, conditions are even worse when they stay awake.

'Do you know what time of the week it is?' they say.

With heavy heart and drooping spirit you reply:

'Yes. It's Friday night.'

'And what happens on Friday night?' they say, fiddling with your pyjama cord and making threatening forays with their thumbs in the nether regions of the popping crease.

'Oh crumbs. All right,' you say. 'But do you mind if I listen to "Today in Parliament"?'

That is the most unbearable ghastliness of 'the physical side' of marriage.

I tell you, dear readers, with all the seriousness I can muster, that if I had my way there would be a close season for it as there is in coarse fishing, and, if anyone were caught indulging in it out of season, they would be heavily fined and have their tackle confiscated.

And on that note I rest my case in support of apartheid.

Long may it flourish.

Long may the sexes remain strictly segregated.

And, if they do have to meet for the propagation of the species, it must be done under licence on the strict understanding that it is done for one purpose and one purpose alone – the finding of a successor to Sir Geoffrey Boycott as opening batsman for England.

23
Blofeld Revisited

The sounds of night deep in the English countryside at Witney Scrotum.

Our batty, splay-foot bard and spinner, Undermilk-wood, warbles at the moon:

'It is spring moonless night, starless and Cordle black, and the hunched woollers' and watkins' wood limps invisible down to. . .'

And at that moment an upstairs window rasps open in the cottage of the village blacksmith, Gooch, and our bard takes refuge as he is peppered with a barrage of composition cricket balls, wicket mallets and the discarded parings of Mr Ian Botham's big toenails (lethal up to 100 yards).

Now there is silence.

Peace.

Then we hear the sly, snuffling feet of the village poacher, Prodger, as he slinks through the darkness towards his traps in the copse at Cowdrey's Bottom.

Owls hoot. Starlings scutter in the eaves. Wild geese cry.

And beside me in the conjugal bed lies the sleeping form of the lady wife, seam up, and a brief smile flickers over those familiar odious, revolting features as we indulge in a spot of mutual tummy rumbling.

I am content.

Memories of a programme on the moving television screen seen earlier in the evening glow in my mind langorously and sensuously.

Brideshead Revisited – what a magnificent story.

The corruption of youth, the decay of innocence, the blighting of high ideals – poor, poor Sebastian Coe.

A tear crinkles the corner of my eye, for I have a similar tale to tell.

It starts many many years ago in the honeyed haze of blissful youth.

But through the haze it stands out clear and sharp.

I see it now.

Still do I recall the poignant pain of my first sight of Blofeld Castle.

We had driven there, Lord Henry Blofeld and I, from Oxford in a friend's Hispano-Pilling open tourer.

The country lanes were warbled and leafy and beside us on the front seat sat Lord Henry's teddy bear, Marloysius.

'Take care he doesn't lose his temper,' said my friend.

And then as the sun mounted high we turned without warning into a cart track and stopped.

And there on a sheep-cropped knoll under a clump of elms we ate strawberries and drank a noble Château Prideaux and smoked fat and languid Ibadulla Turkish cigarettes.

We drove on for another hour or so and then in the early afternoon came to our destination.

Blofeld Castle -- what a sight to behold.

A soaring, extravagant, sumptuous folly of broad windows, golden cupolas, plunging buttresses and flaring balconies, which provoked in me a near mystic trance such as I had experienced on my first sight of the pavilion at Bramall Lane.

'It's where my family live,' said Lord Henry.

And even then, rapt in the vision, I felt momentarily an ominous chill at the words he used.

We sat in the car for a while outside the gates, and he told me in a brooding monotone something of the history of that sublime and eccentric edifice.

It had been built by an ancestor, the rake and dandy, Lord Gower Blofeld.

Lord Gower, known to his friends as 'Lulu' because of his extremely short stature, his exceptionally foul singing voice and his remarkable facial resemblance to Wedekind's grandmother, had been deeply impressed by the riotous and debauched weekends he had spent at Fonthill and Medmenham Abey in the company of the Hellfire Club and its founder, the awesomely notorious Sir Francis Keating.

'Stap me,' he once said. 'They were damn near as licentious and bibacious as a night out in Herne Hill with the Bedser brothers, Alec and Eric.'

Accordingly he determined to take the staid old dank Norman pile of Blofeld Castle and transform it into an exotic fairyland of dark delights and coal black, slow black, crow black wickedness.

He spared no expense on his enterprise.

The finest craftsmen in the land were engaged to take copies of the infamous erotic murals on the BBC commentary box urinals at Trent Bridge.

Master masons were employed to carve representations of the hideously, monstrously contorted faces of the gargoyles on the roof of the Headingley pavilion, depicting incidents at a Yorkshire County Cricket Club annual general meeting.

Great painters were hired to transcribe to the galleries of Blofeld Castle the world's most celebrated salacious masterpieces, including Monet's 'Two Haystacks', a twin portrait of Derek Randall and Alastair Hignell, Gauguin's 'Why Are You Angry?', a delicate and subtly risqué painting of the confrontation between Mr Javed Miandad and Mr Dennis Lillee, and Toulouse-Lautrec's wondrous 'Leicestershire CCC shower room with reclining Ken Higgs'.

At length it was completed, but Lord Gower was not alive to see the masterpiece on which he had lavished his whole fortune.

Prolonged exposure to the cricket reports of Mr Tony Lewis and an unfortunate encounter with an infected cricket bat at the Cheltenham Festival brought him to an early grave and when he died in the arms of his beloved companion, Sir Francis Keating, his last words were:

'When you write my obituary in the Guardian, for Gd's ake mke sure yous pell my nome tight.'

When my friend, Lord Henry, had finished his story, he turned to me suddenly and said savagely through clenched teeth:

'Cricket!'

And once more I felt an icy chill dig deep into my vitals.

But for the moment I was enchanted and bewitched as we drove round the front of the house into a side court and entered through the fortress-like, stone-vaulted passages of the servants' quarters.

'I want you to meet Nanny Grimmett,' said Lord Henry. 'That's what we've come for.'

We pushed open the door of her room, and the old lady turned and said:

'Well, this is a surprise.'

Lord Henry kissed her, but before I had time to take stock of my surroundings she had padded me up, handed me a Gunn and Moore three-springer and given me a strenuous half-hour in the nets.

The fingers were rheumy, the limbs were stiff, but, by God, the old lady could still bowl a damnable googly.

I had to use all my wiles to keep my castle intact.

Lord Henry lounged on a chaise longue and watched the proceedings sulkily.

'Your friend has an excellent lofted on drive,' said Nanny Grimmett. 'Although I fear his stance is too square on to deal effectively with over-pitched seamers on the off stump.'

'Cricket,' said Lord Henry viciously.

Then he sighed long and hard and, taking me by the arm, said:

'Come on. I suppose we had better meet my family.'

It was as we descended the narrow stairs that led from the servants' quarters to the main body of the house and stepped into the main hall and paused awhile that I realized what had been haunting me from the moment I had first entered the confines of Blofeld Castle.

It was everywhere, an overpowering presence, a burning faith that could not be suppressed by decree or by dungeon, by gallows or by axeman's block.

It was an atavistic yearning that coiled and writhed deep in the souls of this ancient and noble family.

It was the faith that defies logic and flourishes riotously and rampantly on blind acceptance of its essential goodness.

It was, of course, cricket.

And its influence was everywhere.

We walked along the corridors and flanking us in rows and rows of glass cases were the exhibits in the world's finest, most comprehensive collection of cricket erotica.

I stopped, bewitched and enchanted, before a case containing the photographs of Mr Patrick Eagar, entitled 'The Nude in County Cricket'.

I saw a hand-tooled copy of the rare first edition of Mr E. W. 'Gloria' Swanton's *A Down and Out in Hove and Tonbridge Wells*.

I gasped in awe at the lead sphere immersed in sterile water embedded in six feet of pre-stressed concrete, which contained a lock of Mr Ian Chappell's pubic hair.

And there next to that was, naughtiness of naughtiness, Mr Fred Rumsey's left sock.

Lord Henry suddenly stopped, opened a door and pushed me inside.

'I suppose you want to see this,' he said.

It took me a few seconds for my eyes to adjust to the light, but when I took in the scene that presented itself to me, I gasped.

We were in a long and narrow room decorated in the arts and crafts style of the last century.

Angels in printed cotton smocks, rambler roses, flower-spangled meadows, frisking lambs, texts in Celtic scripts, saints in armour covered the walls in an intricate pattern of clear, bright colours.

'What is it?' I said.

'It's the indoor batting school,' said Lord Henry.

'Golly,' I said.

'It was Papa's wedding present to Mama,' said my friend.

We left the room in silence.

Many years later I was to repaint its walls with scenes in the life of Winston Place, including 'The Late Cutting of D.V.P. Wright'.

Later that evening over dinner I was to meet the rest of the Blofeld family.

Lord Henry's mother, the Duchess, greeted us warmly.

'Do tell us all the news,' she said. 'Is dear "Tich" Freeman still tweaking the crimson rambler? Is "Patsy" Hendren still wearing his divinely silly hats?'

As we tucked into the plovers' eggs and the quail's toenails Lord Henry's youngest sister, Cordelia, clapped her hands and burbled excitedly:

'I must know. Will Harold Gimblett ever play for England? Oh, do say he will, Henry.'

And all the while the heavy features of Lord Henry's eldest brother, Birdy, were fixed on me in a morass of lumbering puzzlement under the peak of the flat white cap which he wore constantly both indoors and out, giving him an appearance as attractive as a condemned cooling tower.

At length he spoke.

'I am deeply puzzled,' he said. 'It is the laws of the game. Take law 20 – Lost Ball. I quote:

'"If a ball in play cannot be found any fieldsman may call Lost Ball when 6 runs shall be added to the score: but if more than 6 runs have been run before Lost Ball is called, as many runs as have been completed shall be scored. The run in progress shall count provided that the batsmen have crossed at the instant of the call Lost Ball."'

He shook his head slowly.

'Lost Ball?' he said. 'How can a ball ever be deemed Lost, if one acknowledges the existence of an all powerful omniscient God?'

'Oh crumbs, Birdy, don't be such an old Jesuit,' said Cordelia. 'It's the way the game's played that's important. The rules don't matter a fig.'

'They do to me,' said Birdy gloomily.

We repaired to the drawing room and there the Duchess read to us.

She had a beautiful voice and great humour of expression.

She read part of *The Lyfe and Good Deedes of Brian*

Bolus by the Blessed St John Stevas and extracts from *Biggles Plays for Worcestershire*.

It was a day I was to remember all my life, even though it ended on a note of enigma and bitterness.

As we sat smoking in Lord Henry's bedroom late into the night, my friend turned to me and said with a venom I had not suspected existed in his gentle and sensitive soul:

'My God, how I hate cricket.'

And then he smiled wanly and said:

'And so does papa. That is his one saving grace.'

Papa!

The fourteenth Duke of Wisden!

What a man!

What a tragedy, for in him resided the malodorous roots of the cancer which finally sucked the lifeblood from his family.

I was soon to discover exactly why.

It was Lord Henry Blofeld's custom to travel abroad during the months of winter.

Although there was no need for him to do so financially, he was in the habit for the good of his soul to fill in his time in foreign climes by writing abstruse and recondite articles for the *Manchester Guardian* and the *Sunday Express*.

So it was one late autumn evening he said to me as we lay nude on the roof of the nursery idly filling in order forms for greenhouses and garden sheds in the *Radio Times*:

'Come with me to Venice. I need someone to hold my india rubber.'

I jumped at the opportunity.

'We shall visit papa,' said Lord Henry. 'You'll adore him, I promise.'

I remember very little of the train journey to Venice, for during most of the journey I was incarcerated in the ablutions offices laid low by a violent attack of the dreaded Nawab of Pataudis.

We arrived at Venice in the early morning and were conducted by gondola to the Duke of Wisden's residence, the Palazzio Dexter.

The Duke greeted me with courtesy and an amused gravity of mien. His son he kissed full on the lips, and I remember feeling embarrassment, for in my family the only living creature my father ever kissed was his bald and toothless border terrier, Cotton.

My embarrassment was increased some time later, when, having dressed for dinner, I encountered in the drawing room a woman of quivering glamour and deep, sensuous mystery.

The Duke of Wisden introduced me to her quite baldly:

'This is my mistress, Mrs Lane. You must call her Carla.'

She smiled at me and touched me lightly on the knee.

In an instant my stomach was churned to butterflies, and I knew that if she had ordered me to do so, I should have agreed to fly solo round the world on the back of a one-winged Liver bird.

I recall not one thing of dinner, for I was overpowered by the grandeur and dignity of the Duke of Wisden and overwhelmed by the beauty of his mistress, Mrs Lane.

I could scarcely wait to change into my dressing gown

and wrench from Lord Henry, as we sat on his balcony overlooking the silken dusk shrouding the Grand Canal in her flimsy shifts of rose and violet, every detail of his father's 'past'.

My friend was genuinely surprised about my ignorance and launched with vigour into the story of his father's 'disgrace'.

This in a nutshell is what he told me:

The Duke of Wisden was the central figure in the great abdication crisis of 1922.

It appears that one of the grand hereditary titles of state granted to the Wisden family was the presidency of the MCC.

On the death of his father in 1922 the Duke of Wisden should have acceded to that exalted office, but for two crucial impediments – one, he loathed and despised cricket, and, two, he had fallen in love with a divorced lady, who, worse still, was American and, chagrin of chagrin, was a lover of baseball.

The Duke's lack of knowledge of and sympathy with cricket could have been circumvented for, after all, so many administrators of our 'summer game' have set a firm precedent on that matter.

The presence of Mrs Lane, however, and the Duke of Wisden's firm refusal to terminate his relationship with her, was an insuperable obstacle.

The 'highest in the land' pleaded with him to change his mind.

The King went down on bended knees.

The Archbishop of Canterbury preached impassioned sermons in pulpits the length and breadth of the country.

Questions were asked of Mr Robin Day and Sir David Jacobs.

The Prime Minister even went so far as to present a list of suitable candidates whom the government would be prepared to accept as his mistress.

'No, no, no,' bellowed the Duke of Wisden. 'Never, never shall I share my bed with Mr K. D. "Slasher" MacKay of Queensland and Australia.'

The result was inevitable – the abdication of 1922 and the Duke's banishment in disgrace from the land of his birth.

'So there you have it, my dear,' said Lord Henry.

'Golly,' I said.

Two days later I was summoned back to London to embark upon a career of service to King and country which was to take me to some of the most outlandish parts of our blessed and noble Empire.

It was the last I was to see of my friend, for in the early years of the 1960s I learned that he had met his end violently during the mass outbreak of bed-wetting among Australian fast bowlers and putative critics of the moving television screen.

Some say he was kicked to death by the first change seamer of Queensland.

Some say he drank himself to death on linseed oil in Melbourne.

I myself prefer the theory that he was bored to death by Mr Clive James in Sydney.

As for the Duke, I last met him under the most curious of circumstances.

I chanced to be passing by Blofeld Castle on my way in the trusty Lanchester to Cardiff, where the lady wife was in the habit of taking boxing lessons from Mr Joe Erkskine.

On an impulse I decided to 'call in'.

I was met by a scene of grief and desolation.

Cordelia it was who told me that three weeks previously the Duke of Wisden had arrived totally unexpectedly at Blofeld Castle and announced to his family that he had come home to die.

He had repaired immediately to the great state bedroom with its bas-reliefs of the laying down of the covers at Bramall Lane, its ornate baroque ceiling adrift with nymphs and cherubs, seraphs and Gloucester stumpers, its golden statuettes of St Christopher Martin-Jenkins, and there he lay, placid and content to await his death.

'It's a damn nuisance really,' said Birdy. 'The Square's crying out for its first cut of the season, and we just can't get the gang mower out from under his bed.'

'No, no, no, it's far worse than that,' cried Cordelia. 'Papa is so close to death, and yet still he will not repent. Still he will not allow himself to be converted to cricket.'

I shook my head solemnly.

I asked to be allowed to see him as he lay on his death bed.

'I don't see why not,' said Birdy. 'Everyone else seems to be there.'

Indeed they were.

Standing in silent clusters round his bed were the friends in 'high places' summoned by the Duchess in a fruitless effort to obtain the death-bed conversion.

I saw the Archbishop of Canterbury, Dr Gerald Priestland, the Moderator of the Free Church of Lancashire, the Rev. Donald Mosey, the Roman Catholic Bishop of Lords, the Very Rev. Dom Brian Johnston and the Archbishop of Wales and Pebble Mill, Dr Tony Lewis.

The Duke's eyes were closed when I entered the room, but as I approached the bed, they opened, and he extended his arms towards me.

'Go to him, I beg of you,' whispered the Duchess. 'He has been in the deepest of trances this past five days. It is as though he had been watching an opening partnership by Sir Geoffrey Boycott and Mr Christopher Tavare.'

I moved closer to his bed.

The congregation was still and silent as I leaned towards him.

His voice was weak and cracked, but within its soul I detected a burning spirit that would not be assuaged.

'I have been to the other side,' he said. 'I have seen paradise.'

Silence.

The clock ticked.

The Rev. Mosey and Dom Brian Johnston changed places in the commentary box.

The Duchess nodded to me urgently.

I spoke softly.

'And what was it like?'

A great and beautific smile spread over his careworn but still handsome features.

He spoke.

'I think it's going to be a sticky dog,' he said.

And then his eyes closed, his breathing stopped and his stumps were finally drawn by the celestial Umpire in the heavens.

The rejoicing of his family and his friends was staggering to behold.

They wept.

They sang.

They prayed.

They danced.

At last he had been 'converted'.

I slipped out quietly.

And as I drove down the long driveway I stopped the car and turned my eyes for the last time towards Blofeld Castle.

I saw Nanny Grimmett supervising a session in the nets.

I saw Birdy driving the gang mower in great swathes up and down the square waving wildly his flat white cap.

And I am pretty certain, although, of course, I cannot be sure, that I saw rising towards the heavens the soul of the Duke of Wisden.

It was conveyed in a cricket bag.

And on its side, written in letters of shimmering gold, were the following words:

'Sponsored by Nat West Bank Ltd.'

24
Cricket Ahoy

It is my firm and unshakeable belief that for lovers of our dear and blessed 'summer game' cruising by ocean liner could be made tolerable by one simple change in operations.

It is this:

The vessel should remain firmly at anchor in its home port for the whole duration of the voyage.

What the wallahs at cruising HQ wilfully fail to recognize is that it is totally unnecessary to entertain the voyagers with visits to loathsome foreign countries, swarming with greasy wops, foul-smelling Greeks, sex-crazed Spaniards and lascivious, free-loading travel writers for the *Sunday Times*.

What sane, right-thinking, civilized man could possibly feel the need for lectures by pansy flower arrangers and cabaret turns by Cardew Robertson and female go-go dancers with bad breath and fat ankles?

Good God, within a handy radius of the port of Southampton there are at least six first-class county cricket grounds.

Why go to all the trouble and all the expense of 'carting' us off to foreign climes when all the entertainment a man of discernment needs is on his very doorstep?

It is quite clear to me, anyway, that the vast majority of passengers on a cruise liner are there against their will.

The most cursory examination of the wretches is enough to convince me that they have been press-ganged from the scummiest, waterfront flesh pots of the East End of London and the foullest pits of the industrial cities of the North.

I confess, dear readers, I feel sorry for them.

They have been shoved into ill-fitting dinner jackets and shapeless evening frocks which are quite obviously alien to their normal mode of dress.

Deprived of their natural daily diet of fish and chips and mentholated catarrh pastilles, they sit helplessly at the dinner table wondering which fork to use on their salmi of pheasant à la mode Harry Makepeace.

And for most of the time while the vessel is at sea they are depositing the contents of their stomachs in cascades of vomit, for which there can be no possible excuse – dear Lord, no one is compelling them to read the cricket reports of Mr Tony Lewis.

These gloomy and sombre reflections descend upon me as I think back to a cruise forced upon me by the lady wife in the late summer of last year.

Sheer, unadulterated misery and torture.

The only crumb of comfort was the fact that the lady wife's confounded Bedlington terriers were placed in kennels for the duration of the voyage and returned home in some distress have being bitten several times on their respective rumps by the proprietress of the establishment.

Obviously a woman of some refinement with a splendid pair of choppers to boot.

However, for the rest of the experience the only sobriquet I can offer is a quotation from the immortal prose of Mr E. R. 'Elizabeth Regina' Dexter – 'absolutely rotten'.

Even now I shudder with horror as I recall that fatal day when the lady wife 'trapped' me.

The morning had started with such promise.

The post brought the lady wife the intelligence that her loathsome spinster sister in Cheltenham would be unable to make her annual visit to us owing to her parrot's going down with avian bunions.

Even better things were to follow.

The lesser spotted woodpecker visited the lawn, the milkman with the noisy thumbs was extensively savaged by the commodore's geese, and the 'Freezer Special' was cancelled on the Jimmy Young Radio Show.

Freezer Special?

Dear oh dear, what on earth is the wireless coming to?

All one receives on it these days are the unctuous tones of Roy Plomley and constant interference from Mavis Nicholson.

It has never been the same for me since the blessed Wilfred Pickles was taken from us and translated to that great Haywood's factory in the sky.

None the less, I was content that morning as I watched the lady wife slapping vast quantities of greengage jam on her cowering slice of toast for all the world like a hairy Portsmouth matelot daubing his underpants with protective tallow.

Suddenly she looked up at me and spoke the following words:

'I am not going to Scarborough this year.'

Can you imagine the happiness which flooded over me?

Dear readers, what was in prospect?

A week entirely on my own in the most splendid watering place on the whole North Yorkshire coast.

A week entirely dedicated to cricket, snorters, and sleeping in my socks.

No lady wife criticizing the breakfast sausages and dragging me off to the theatre each evening to watch the completely unintelligible plays of that profound stinker, Alan Ayckman.

Why he couldn't stick to playing cricket for Sussex instead of writing plays about people eating pilchards in bed, I shall never know.

I am not a prejudiced man, but if I had my way I should take the whole vile band of Scarborough summer entertainers and compel them to sit through half an hour of Max Jaffa and when they came out screaming for mercy, I should mow them down with a gatling gun and drop their corpses off the top of Oliver's Mount, and, if any of them survived that, I should inflict upon them the ultimate of ultimate horrors – a quarter of an hour in the presence of the Krankies.

Where was I?

Ah yes, the breakfast table.

I looked up at the lady wife, and I smiled sweetly, and I said:

'What's that you said, my dear?'

She looked at me with those piggy little eyes of hers glinting and her face breaking into a grin like a crack on a Brisbane 'sticky dog'.

'I said, I am not going to Scarborough this year,' she said. 'And neither are you.'

'What?'

'Neither of us is going to Scarborough,' said the lady wife. 'I have booked a cruise instead.'

In vain did I plead with her.

For a whole week I hung round the entrance to the village school at Witney Scrotum during the annual attack of measles.

Not a single spot.

For three days I stood out in the garden in the rain totally nude except for souwester and MCC spats.

Not a single snuffle.

I feigned malaria, beri-beri, piles, rickets, trench fever, rinderpest, gapes, heaves, staggers, scurvy, hog cholera and a terminal attack of the dreaded Nawab of Pataudis.

All to no avail – the lady wife would not budge.

And thus did we find ourselves that fateful Friday

evening trudging up the gangplank of a vessel whose name I did not quite catch.

I had an immediate altercation as soon as I set foot on board when some shifty-eyed Lascar attempted to wrench my cricket bag from my grasp.

'Take your hands off,' I bellowed. 'Don't you realize that in that bag I carry all the articles essential to health and happiness for a voyage at sea? – the complete waterproof set of *Wisden's Almanack*, three packets of disposable abdominal protectors and a self-righting, inflatable smoker's compendium?'

Worse was to follow when I was damn near garrotted by streamers flung from the deck as we departed from Southampton.

I gave the offender, a gormless lout in lime-green moleskin trilby and maroon Bermuda shorts, a swift cuff round the earhole and repaired to the bar, where I spent the remainder of the evening reaming my pipe and glowering at the nancy boy waiters with their gold earrings and false suntans.

The following day was made faintly tolerable by the lady wife's being confined to quarters as we crossed the Bay of Biscay, and I was thus able to spill my kedgeree on my lap at leisure under the benign, brown-eyed gaze of the excellent Goanese waiter, who, incidentally bore a marked resemblance to Mr Leo Brittan, although I found his accent infinitely easier to understand.

Two days out and what appeared to be a bright, shining shaft of light to send my spirits soaring was of an instant doused, and I was once more plunged into gloom and despair.

The circumstances were thus:

While taking my early morning stroll on deck I encountered a man dressed entirely from head to foot in white.

Good God, I thought to myself, civilization at last.

I approached him jauntily, slapped him on the back and said:

'Whatho. Typical of the trash who organize this cruise not to tell us they've arranged a cricket match. Playing the dagos when we get to Casablanca, are we?'

He looked at me silently for a moment.

And then he said:

'Sir, I am the captain.'

'Even better,' I said. 'My services are at your disposal. I am a moderately secure middle order batsman and I am no mean hand when it comes to tweaking the googly.'

A massive scowl came to his vile face.

'I am not the captain of a cricket team, sir,' he said. 'I am the captain of the ship.'

'In that case, my dear sir,' I replied, 'get back upstairs and start driving the bloody thing.'

With what misery I repaired to the bar.

Fond hopes dashed.

The cup of happiness snatched from my lips by the cruel hands of fate.

I was desolate.

My whisky tasted like sewing machine oil.

My cigar tasted like the end of the exhaust pipe on a Co-op coal cart.

The potato crisps tasted like damp raffle tickets.

And then I spotted him.

He was sitting on his own, surreptiously appending

moustaches to the faces of the ladies on the mural entitled: 'Aphrodite and Handmaidens Fleeing from the Grasp of Alan Jones at Swansea – Glamorgan versus Worcestershire.'

It was a familiar face.

It was a very familiar face.

It was.

It wasn't.

It couldn't be.

By thunder, it was.

'Tufty Stackpole,' I bellowed at the top of my voice.

He started and spilled a tray of curried rice crispies down the front of his I Zingari dungarees.

A great smile of warmth and good humour came to his face.

'Good God,' he said. 'It's you.'

I pumped his hand and clasped his shoulders.

I had discovered a long lost friend.

I had not seen him for all of forty-three years when he had returned home from Burma 'in disgrace' after an incident involving a slip catching cradle, three members of the band of Troise and his Mandoliers and a portion of Sir Geoffrey Boycott's punkah.

'Tufty Stackpole,' I said warmly. 'By God, you've turned into the spitting image of Mary O'Hara. I hope your voice sounds better, though.'

Snorters were instantly ordered.

Snorters were instantly dispatched down gullets glowing with mutual friendships.

'Tufty Stackpole,' I said, smacking him on the thighs. 'What the devil are you doing on this loathsome cattle boat?'

He ordered a bottle of fine old vintage Brown and Robertson tawny port, and, as we sipped that noble liquid washed down with ice cold bottles of Umrigar's Fully Authorized and Harmonious Indian Exhibition Pale Ale, he told me the reason for his presence on the vessel.

He was to pay his annual visit to the cricketers' church at Casablanca.

'Cricketers' church, Tufty?' I said. 'What in the name of blitheration is a church like that doing in the heart of dago land?'

Tufty smiled and patting me softly on the knee said:

'I trust you will accompany me tomorrow when we dock, and there I will explain more fully the nature of my mission.'

'Rather, Tufty,' I said. 'Rather, old hoof.'

The strength of my good mood was further increased when the lady wife informed me over dinner that on the morrow she proposed to take a shore excursion by motor charabanc to visit the site of some ancient Berber burial chambers, the pictures of which looked remarkably like the gents urinals at Bradford Park Avenue.

'I don't suppose you want to come,' she said.

I said that under normal circumstances nothing would give me greater pleasure, but, owing to a slight attack of goat glanders and the threat of impending athlete's foot, I felt it would be unwise to venture into the interior without copious supplies of filtered water, oxygen, sulphur tablets and charcoal biscuits, which I was certain the vile dagos would be unable or unwilling to provide.

The lady wife arched her eyebrows and said nothing.

My mood of euphoria grew in intensity as the evening progressed and was not to be assuaged despite my being forced to attend a cabaret, which to my untutored eye seemed to consist entirely of arthritic jugglers and female singers with big ears.

After this odious event the lady wife marched me to the rear of the ship, where I was compelled to take part in a quiz game.

Why anyone should want to know the name of the capital of Nicaragua is totally beyond me.

And what possible good can come from knowing the identity of the longest suspension bridge in Europe and the author of Mrs Gaskell?

I apprised the quiz master of my views at some length and volunteered to take over the whole foul affair and conduct the quiz on matters of a serious nature – to wit, questions from my 1934 *Wisden's Almanack*.

The pomaded little nancy boy threatened to fetch the master-at-arms, a suggestion which prompted the lady wife to square up to the snivelling wretch and arch her eyebrows.

Calm was restored immediately.

I slept well that night and next morning went on deck as the liner entered harbour through clouds of powdered cement belching from some malodorous quayside factory, which seemed to me to typify the whole of the dago attitude to life.

The lady wife disembarked with her companions and enbussed on a motor charabanc driven by a rascally looking fellow with slant eyes and oily features, who bore a marked resemblance to Mr Leo Brittan, as indeed

I was later to discover did every citizen, male and female alike, of Casablanca.

Tufty and I waited until the activity on the quay had ceased and the hordes of dagos in Tommy Cooper fezes and Marks and Spencers nightshirts had departed to their stinking hovels.

We then strode down the gangplank, hailed a taxi and set forth towards our destination, which I was to find enchanting, enthralling and most deeply moving.

The cricketers' church of St Robin of the Blessed Marlars lies in a quiet backwater just off the main Muhammed V Square, Casablanca's equivalent to the square at our beloved Bramall Lane.

As we walked through the gate in the high stone wall and entered the rose-scented courtyard with its avenues of willows and oaks and its small immaculate lawns enclosed by miniature bushes of box and privet, tears sprang to my eyes.

Here in the very heart of dago land was a spot that was unmistakably, irrefutably English.

How moving.

How the cockles of my heart were warmed.

How my shins throbbed and my elbows quivered.

We did not speak, Tufty and I.

We walked along the cool, gravelled path, pausing from time to time to examine the inscriptions on the gravestones.

'A Yorkshire Professional – Washed Ashore – 1913.'

'D. J. K. Begby – Captain of Berkshire, 1878 – Died of Infections too Numerous to Mention.'

'L. R. Stopford – Died At Sea While en Route to Tour Sierra Leone with MCC – his Batting and Occasional Leg Spinners were Much Missed by All.'

And, most moving of all, in a sweet-scented glade, eleven simple white crosses with a plaque on a marble base bearing the inscription:

'An Unknown Touring English Cricket Party – Massacred by Riff Tribesmen, 1876 – Buried in Full Batting Order.'

With tears coursing down my eyes I was led by my chum into the church.

Here in the soft-flickering twilight he explained all.

The church had been established in the early years of the last century by MCC missionaries to give comfort and succour to cricketers en route to foreign climes and to pilgrims en route to worship at Lords.

Over the years it had been visited by famous and humble alike.

There carved on the reredos I saw the legend:

'D. R. Jardine Loves Gracie Fields.'

And there on the back of the second row of pews I saw carved:

'Bill Frindall can't count – Trevor Bailey.'

In silence we inspected the brass and mahogany memorials and then my chum led me to the innermost sanctuary and there he pointed to a stone memorial in the shape of three wickets with the off bail lying at their feet.

On it was written:

'In Memory of the Rev. H. H. "Foxy" Stackpole erstwhile Stumper and Cleric – Died of Whisky, 1911.'

Tufty lowered his head and I followed suit.

'My father,' he whispered.

And then in a hesitant voice, racked with emotion he told me 'the story'.

Long long ago his father had committed a mortal sin in the Church of MCC.

He had cast doubts upon the divine infallibity of Mr E. W. 'Gloria' Swanton.

He had been banished forthwith to Casablanca and there he had eked out his lonely years comforted only by loose women, the distant and faint commentaries of Mr Don Mosey and bottles of Glen Ranji whisky.

'My condolences, Tufty,' I said.

He shook his head.

He could not speak.

And then a most curious thing happened.

Stepping forward to the memorial, he pulled out the leg stump from its base, unscrewed its top and offered it to me.

'Go on,' he said. 'It's fully of whisky.'

'Whisky?' I said.

'My father's bequest,' said Tufty. 'I have been coming every year since 1932 to drink it. There's only a quarter of the leg stump left.'

And so in silence and comradeship we drank the last of Tufty's bequest.

Later, much later, in the evening we returned to the quayside only to discover that the ship had left without us.

I looked at Tufty.

Tufty looked at me.

'Come on,' he said. 'Let's finish off the off bail.'

We did.

How I got back for Scarborough in time for the last two days of the cricket week is another story.